D0915217

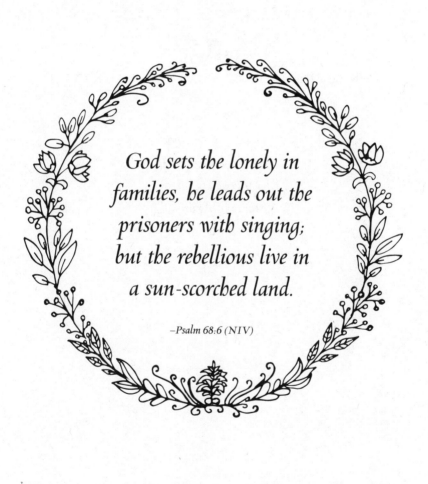

God sets the lonely in
families, he leads out the
prisoners with singing;
but the rebellious live in
a sun-scorched land.

–Psalm 68:6 (NIV)

MYSTERIES *of* LANCASTER COUNTY

THE TIES THAT BIND

MYSTERIES *of* LANCASTER COUNTY

Janice Thompson

Guideposts

New York

THE TIES THAT BIND

DEDICATION

To weary wanderers in search of home...

Blessed be the tie that binds
Our hearts in Christian love;
The fellowship of kindred minds
Is like to that above.

When we asunder part,
It gives us inward pain;
But we shall still be joined in heart,
And hope to meet again.

–John Fawcett

CHAPTER ONE

A n early-morning breeze whipped through the trees out-side of Secondhand Blessings. Elizabeth stood in the open doorway of the shop and took it all in. Her breath caught in her throat as she watched the first colorful leaves of the season float through the air and then tumble to the ground in a crisp, dazzling display of red, gold, and orange. Was there anything finer than October in Lancaster County?

"You might want to close that door before those leaves blow inside." Her younger sister Martha's voice sounded from behind her. "Then we'll have a mess to clean up."

"Sorry." Elizabeth stepped inside, and the door closed. "Just couldn't help myself. I feel like it's been years since I wit-nessed anything this exquisite. God is on full display during harvest season, wouldn't you say?"

"Yes, and the leaves are beautiful," Martha agreed. "I'll give you that. But they're hard enough to rake up outside, let alone inside. The last thing we need is another mess to pick up in here. Those kids yesterday practically tore the place apart. I thought I'd never get the shelves reorganized." She tended to a lantern that was sitting too close to the end of a shelf. "Folks need to keep a closer eye on their kids. That's all I've got to say about that."

"True." Elizabeth walked behind the front counter and tucked her purse on the shelf below the cash register. She couldn't help but smile as her youngest sister, Mary, entered the shop and stood in the open doorway, gushing over the leaves.

"Have you ever?" Mary clasped her hands to her chest. "Oh, they're glorious! And that breeze just takes my breath away. I feel like God just allowed me to glimpse a little foretaste of what heaven's going to be like."

"I, for one, am praying there are no rakes in heaven." Martha clucked her tongue as she walked their way, broom in hand. "Now close that door, Mary. You're letting leaves in. And it's chilly out there."

"Oh, who cares?" Mary giggled and spread her arms wide as a delicious breeze whipped the leaves into a dance that landed several of them squarely inside the shop. "Oops." She looked at Martha. "Don't worry, I'll take care of those." She took the broom from her sister's hand and began to sweep, humming "All Things Bright and Beautiful" as she worked.

Martha brushed a loose strand of hair behind her ear and turned toward the back of the store. "If anyone needs me, I'll be in the stockroom. I've got to catch up on inventory."

Elizabeth arranged several items on the front shelf then paused to watch Mary sweep leaves. Her sister continued to hum as she worked. After a moment Mary stopped sweeping, and a dreamy look came over her. She glanced Elizabeth's way.

"I think Anna picked the perfect season to get married. I just love autumn weddings."

"Me too." Elizabeth thought about their old friend's upcoming nuptials. "And I'm sure you and Martha will do a fine job coordinating everything for her. I'm just glad she asked the two of you and not me. I don't think I would have the time or the inclination."

"I plan to make the time. Anna deserves the very best." Mary released a sigh. "She's waited so long for Mr. Right. When you've held on until your midfifties to get married for the first time, you deserve the full regalia."

Elizabeth did her best not to read too much into her sister's words or to let sad memories overtake her. She'd come pretty close to having a wedding herself. Only her story had taken a turn in the end, one that did not land her at the altar. Shaking off her ponderings, she responded to Mary's comment. "I'm not so sure I'd go all out, even if I'd waited for years. I'd probably go for simple and sweet."

Simple and sweet suited her, she had to admit. Not her sisters, though. Mary and Martha were birds of a different feather, more prone to contemporary dress and style. Mary, especially, kept up to date on the latest fashions and trends. They were certainly the best ones to help Anna prepare for her big day.

"I think Anna's going to ask for the moon, and I'll do my best to give it to her." The edges of Mary's lips tipped up in a comfortable smile. "If you'd told me a year ago I'd be coordinating a wedding, I would have said you were crazy."

Just as quickly, her smile faded, and Elizabeth wondered if Mary was revisiting her broken heart. She wouldn't blame her.

"If you'd told me a year ago we'd be running this shop together, I would have said you were crazy," Elizabeth countered. "But here we are, doing all of the above."

"And loving every minute of it." Mary went back to work, her humming now in full force. "Life has given me lemons, but I've made lemonade."

Elizabeth couldn't help but agree. The rustic old barn had been transformed into a thing of beauty—a shop where people came from far and wide to purchase quaint items. Many items, like the Amish quilts and other hand-sewn crafts, were one of a kind. Their Amish friends and neighbors also supplied them with canned jellies and jams, honey, furniture, and other woodcrafts to sell on consignment. Then there were the secondhand items, the eclectic estate and garage sale gems that kept some customers browsing for hours.

Elizabeth spent the next few minutes prepping the store for customers. Things were in full swing at Secondhand Blessings now that autumn was upon them. More and more folks were coming to their little village of Bird-in-Hand in hopes of finding the perfect Christmas gift. Many, like yesterday's big group, arrived at the remodeled barn with small children in tow. Even though there was a children's area in the center of the shop, complete with small tables and chairs, books, toys, wooden puzzles, and coloring books and crayons, the children ran through the aisles pulling toys off the shelves. The parents didn't seem to mind, but Elizabeth certainly did. So did Martha, apparently. Hopefully today would prove to be calmer.

Elizabeth walked the aisles and straightened the shelves, taking note of their lower-than-usual inventory. Thank goodness they still had an ample supply of handcrafted Amish quilts and crafts. Otherwise she might be a bit concerned, what with Christmas coming and all.

"It's five till ten." Martha's voice rang out from the back of the shop. "Don't forget to flip the sign, Elizabeth."

"Got it." Elizabeth walked to the front door and turned the sign to OPEN. Her gaze landed on a red truck pulling into the parking lot, a Ford F-150 with mud flaps. Something about it seemed familiar. The owner backed the vehicle into a nearby space with ease, giving Elizabeth a clear view of its bumper. A sticker of an American flag caught her attention, along with the words SEMPER FI. This truck must belong to a marine.

Just as she was about to turn back to tidying work, a beautiful black and tan boxer leaped out of the back of the truck and landed on the gravel below. He stood erect, ears perked and hind legs extended, as if awaiting a judge's approval at a dog show. He had one of those scrunchy faces only a mother could love. And the white paws and underbelly were a stunning contrast to the black and tan. He wore a dark green collar, a broad one, suited to his larger physique, but wasn't leashed. Hopefully that wouldn't turn out to be a problem.

Elizabeth stepped outside and took a couple of tentative steps toward the handsome boxer, hoping he was safe to approach. The pooch seemed fine. His docked tail wagged in anticipation, and he let out a couple of hearty barks as she moved his way.

"Rocky, wait for me." Elizabeth glanced up to see the owner of the voice, probably in his midthirties, exiting the cab of the truck. The man pulled off his tattered baseball cap and ran his fingers through his messy brown hair then stuck the cap back on…backward. Only then did Elizabeth notice his golden tan. Interesting, considering the time of year. Maybe he worked outside, in construction or something like that. Or perhaps he was a farmer.

He reached inside the truck and grabbed a leash, which he clipped to the dog's collar. He squatted in front of the dog and rubbed its ears for a minute before standing and closing the door of the cab.

Not wanting to appear nosy, Elizabeth walked back into the store. She fought the temptation to peek over her shoulder. Instead, she tended to some crumbs on the countertop, brushing them into her open palm and dumping them into the trash can. The bell above the door jingled as the man entered the shop with the dog beside him. In his arms he carried a package wrapped in brown paper.

"Okay to bring Rocky inside?" the man called out before taking a step in Elizabeth's direction.

"Um, sure." Her gaze shot to the back of the store. Martha would likely have a fit, but she hated to shoo this man off. Besides, the dog seemed to be friendly enough. Boxers were known to be great with people and nonagressive, most of the time, anyway.

A broad smile stretched across the man's face as he took a couple of steps in her direction. "Thanks. He might look tough, but Rocky's gentle as a lamb. He won't hurt anything."

No sooner had he spoken the words than the dog attempted a getaway. The feisty canine pulled hard against the leash, nearly causing the man to drop the package in his arms. He managed to hold on to both the package and the dog, but Rocky's yelps must have caught the attention of Mary, who came bolting their way.

Her eyes widened when she saw the dog. "Everything okay up here?"

"Yes, ma'am." The man shifted the package in his arms. "Rocky's just testing my patience today. That's not like him, but he's been through a rough time lately."

"Want me to watch him while you shop?" Mary's eyes sparkled as she knelt down to scratch the pooch behind the ears. "Dogs love me, and the feeling's mutual."

"Sure, if you don't mind." He set the package down on the counter and held the leash out to her.

"I don't mind a bit." Mary took the leash and clucked her tongue. "C'mon, boy. Let's go outside for a walk." She stepped outside just in time for a breeze to blow in another round of leaves. "It's beautiful out today!" Mary disappeared into the parking lot, the door closing behind her.

Elizabeth turned her attention to the man across the counter. For the first time she noticed that his hat wasn't the only thing that was tattered. His plaid shirt had seen better days and so had his jeans, with their frayed knees. She did her best to focus on his face, but the frown lines and wrinkled forehead made her even more curious than before. This poor fellow wore the exhaustion of life on his face, especially around the eyes. Strange for one so young.

"How can I help you?" Elizabeth pasted on a bright smile.

"Well, I saw the sign out front, that you take items on consignment. I was hoping I could place this piece right here. I've had it for years." He pulled back the brown wrapping paper to reveal a gorgeous antique pitcher—ivory with lovely rose-colored flowers etched in gold.

Elizabeth ran her finger along the scalloped porcelain, mesmerized by its beauty. "It's lovely," she said after a moment. She flipped it over and glanced at the logo on the bottom. She didn't recognize the name as one she'd seen before.

"Yep," he responded. "We've had it for years."

"And you're sure you want to sell it?" Elizabeth asked.

He nodded.

She knew better than to argue with a customer over such things. Many times she'd wondered how people could part with items they'd owned for years, but it wasn't hers to question.

"Do you have the washbasin?" she asked. "It will fetch a better price with both pieces."

For a moment the man didn't respond. He seemed to lose himself to his thoughts. He finally shrugged. "Nope. Sorry. This is all I've got. But I figure someone will want it."

"Right." She lifted the pitcher and gave it a closer look. Goodness. This would bring in a pretty penny with its basin, but without it…she couldn't be sure. After pondering the issue for a moment, Elizabeth offered a compromise. "Tell you what. Instead of taking it on consignment, why don't I just purchase it from you outright? That way you won't have to wait for your money. I'm sure the right buyer will come along." And even if they didn't, she would still purchase the pitcher from this man as a thank-you for his service to their country.

"Sure, sounds good." A hint of a smile tipped up the edges of the man's lips, and relief flooded his eyes. "I appreciate it."

"No worries. Would thirty dollars work for you?"

"Sure. Sounds good," he said again.

Mary came bolting back through the automatic door with the dog leading the way. "He's very—" The dog ran down the center aisle, nearly knocking over a holiday display. "Fast!" Mary called out from the back of the store.

A crash sounded just as Elizabeth pulled cash from the register to hand to the man. He took the bills then sprang into action to fetch the dog. Moments later he returned, the dog in tow. "Looks like I owe you for a farmhouse cookie jar that Rocky knocked over."

"Nah." With the wave of a hand, Elizabeth dismissed that idea. "It was chipped anyway. Been on the shelf for ages, in fact."

"If you're sure." He thanked her and headed toward the door. The dog continued to wag his tail as his owner gave a little tug on the leash. "Let's go, Rocky. Attaboy." Seconds later the door swung open, and they disappeared into the parking lot.

Elizabeth reached for the broom and dustpan then headed to the back of the store to sweep up whatever mess the dog had made. She found Mary kneeling, picking up the larger pieces of glass and depositing them into a small trash can.

"I can help you with that," Elizabeth said. She gestured to the broom. "Thought we might need this."

"Sure." Mary groaned as she stood. "Well, he sure was a handsome dog."

"That's a good word for a boxer...handsome," Elizabeth agreed. "He had beautiful markings."

"True." Mary nodded. "He was a little rowdy, though." She paused. "What did his owner want?"

Before Elizabeth could explain, she noticed Martha heading their way from the office in the back.

"I just had a phone call from—" Martha didn't finish her sentence. Instead, she gazed down at the shattered cookie jar. "What in the world? What did I miss?"

"Oh, just a dog running amok and knocking things over." Elizabeth swept up the remaining bits of glass. "I was getting tired of looking at that old thing anyway. No one was ever going to buy it." She paused. "Now, who was on the phone?"

"Oh, right. Phone." Martha's worry lines deepened. "I'm afraid it was sad news. Bishop Jacob Wittmer has passed away. That was his daughter, Susanna, on the phone. She's asked us to help spread the word to our customers."

"I'm so sorry to hear that." Elizabeth stopped sweeping to acknowledge her sister's announcement. Bishop Wittmer was one of the oldest of all the Amish in their community and well loved by those he served. "I knew he was ill, of course, but certainly didn't expect him to pass away this quickly."

"No one did." Martha placed her hands on her hips. "I've volunteered to take a meal over tomorrow. The extended family will be coming in from all over, and I'm sure they could use something before the day of the service."

"That's nice of you." Elizabeth nodded. "And I'll be happy to help." Anything for a respected member of their tight-knit community.

"Susanna also mentioned an auction this Saturday," Martha added. "She wanted me to know there should be a lot of great pieces we might want for the shop."

"Right." Still, Elizabeth didn't feel like focusing on that at the moment, not with the bishop's passing so fresh in her mind. His death was a great loss to the community. So many loved him dearly.

As she walked to the front of the store, Elizabeth found her thoughts drifting back to the man with the porcelain pitcher. She pondered the creases in his brow, the circles under his eyes. The sadness on his face now matched the feelings in her heart as she pondered the death of one of the community's finest men. Strange how the words on that bumper sticker now seemed to fit the somber news she had just received about a beloved member of their community.

"*Semper Fi*, Bishop Wittmer," Elizabeth whispered. "Always faithful."

CHAPTER TWO

Yoo-hoo!"

Elizabeth looked up as she heard the familiar voice at the door of the shop on Saturday morning. Bride-to-be Anna Bennett gave her a little wave then rushed her way, a bright smile on her face. Elizabeth couldn't help but notice that her childhood friend looked much younger than her fifty-four years. The upcoming nuptials had put a spring in Anna's step and had apparently given her a new fashion sense as well. Anna's brown hair had been styled in a cute new bob, and she was wearing a burgundy blouse and fitted black slacks and heels. Love had that effect on some people, Elizabeth supposed. Or maybe it had more to do with the fact that Anna lived and worked in the big city. She'd traded in her simple life for one with a bit more color.

"I didn't know you were coming in today, Anna." Elizabeth shut the cash register and smiled. "Do Mary and Martha know?"

"Oh yes." Anna beamed. "I called Martha yesterday to tell her about some changes I want to make to the cake design, and she told me this would be a good day to stop by. I hope that's okay."

"Of course. How are things going with the wedding plans?"

"Great! It's been a bit of a challenge to get everything done long-distance. Not that New Jersey is really that far away, of course, but now that I'm back home…" She grinned. "Goodness,

I didn't realize I still considered Bird-in-Hand home after all these years." A chuckle followed. "Anyway, now that I'm home with a full week before the big day, I need to take advantage of every minute. So here I am." Anna plopped a large scrapbook down on the counter and then opened it. She turned it to face Elizabeth.

"What have we got here?"

"I've been putting together pictures for the wedding. What do you think of this cake?" Anna pointed to a picture at the bottom of the page.

Elizabeth tried not to convey her shock as she saw the elaborate multitiered wonder. "Martha's making *that* for you?"

Martha was a great baker, of course, but five tiers of heavily decorated, intricately piped wedding cake? That might be asking a lot.

Anna flipped the pages of the book, and several other pictures came into view. "Oh, I'm not sold on that one, at least not yet. It just happens to be my favorite at the moment. One of the ladies I work with at the hospital had something like that at her wedding, and I fell in love with it. I've already linked Martha to my cake photos on Pinterest. I've got over forty cake pictures stored there." A girlish giggle slipped out, and she closed the scrapbook. "So who knows what I'll end up with? But that's why I'm here." She put her hand up. "I know, I know. Most brides settle on the cake months before the big day. I'm not making this easy on her."

To say the least.

Anna pulled her phone out and opened the Pinterest app to show off some cake design photos. They were all quite elaborate.

"I'm also still talking through the decor with Mary. It's all going to be very rustic. I believe they call it 'farmhouse chic.'"

"I see. So farmhouse is chic now, is it?" Elizabeth couldn't help but laugh. "I don't know if our Amish friends will be happy or mortified to hear they're in fashion."

"Yes, it's quite the thing. Outdoorsy. Lots of hay bales, burlap, mason jars, that sort of thing."

"Sounds quaint."

"Very. I'll be using pumpkins too, since it's October. It's going to be very romantic but casual at the same time. That's why I'm still having trouble settling on a final plan for the cake. It has to go with the rest of the decor. And yet it has to be big enough to feed one hundred and fifty people."

"My goodness. You've invited everyone."

"Pretty much." Anna sighed. "That's one blessing of coming back to Bird-in-Hand to tie the knot. I'll be surrounded by old friends and family. So many of my friends and loved ones will be there. But a lot of our friends from the hospital are coming too, and not just the ladies in the admissions department. Doctors, nurses...they're all going to converge on Bird-in-Hand." She lit into several details about specific friends and family members, and Elizabeth started to feel the conversation might never end.

"You'll definitely need a decent-sized cake, then." Elizabeth glanced at her watch. "I'm not sure how much time Martha can visit though. We're headed to the Wittmers' for the auction in a while, so..."

"I heard about the bishop." Anna's lips turned down in a frown. "So sad. He's been such a fixture in town, for as long as I can remember."

"Yes. I knew he was in bad shape, but figured he still had some time." Elizabeth sighed. "I'm going to miss the way he used to make everyone laugh. It's rare to find an Amish bishop with such a knack for humor."

"Oh, there you are, Anna!" Mary's voice sounded from down the center aisle of the store. She walked their way, hands clasped together. "Martha and I are buzzing with excitement. We're ready to get this show started!"

"Thank you so much for helping out with my big day." Anna closed her scrapbook and smiled. "Just a few loose ends to tie up before I can enjoy my final week of single life."

"Would you like to look around the store first?" Mary asked. "I've put together a list of items that might match your farm-house chic decor. We're happy to loan you whatever you like to make your big day complete. We'll get that old barn looking like a million bucks."

"Sounds wonderful." Anna practically beamed as she glanced around the store. "I'm so grateful, not just for the loan of the items but for your friendship and your help. I couldn't do this without you ladies."

Anna's enthusiasm warmed Elizabeth's heart. What bride wouldn't be excited about her big day? And converting the Bennetts' oversized family barn into a reception hall would be just the ticket.

"I've got a couple of old chandeliers that will be perfect over the cake table," Mary said. "We'll just have to figure out a way to rig them so they're secure."

Judging from the excitement on Anna's face, she found this to be a lovely idea. "Speaking of the cake table, I saw the most amazing picture on Pinterest and knew right away it would be perfect." Anna clasped her hands together. "A table that looks like a wagon. It's basically just a large rustic table with four wagon wheels attached, so it should be pretty easy to put together. My brother is looking for wagon wheels as we speak."

"That sounds perfect," Mary said.

"Oh, and I'm just going crazy with other ideas too. We're going to have all sorts of sweets on the cake table—wedding cookies, lemon bars—you name it. And wait till I tell you about the savory foods we've decided to serve. This is going to be a wedding no one ever forgets."

Elizabeth felt sure Anna could say that twice and mean it. Most folks in these parts didn't go for elaborate, over-the-top celebrations like this, at least not the people Elizabeth knew well. This wedding would definitely stand out.

Not that Mary seemed to mind. In fact, she seemed almost giddy. She took Anna by the arm. "Come with me, Anna. Let's look around the shop and see what else we might be able to spare for your big day. I just remembered a couple of antique lanterns that will be perfect to display on that table you've described."

They headed off to the back of the store together, chattering like schoolgirls. Elizabeth waited until they were out of sight to sigh aloud as she turned her attention back to the register. Oh well. Someone had better keep an eye on the shop while the ladies focused on wedding planning.

The next hour she waited on dozens of customers. Most Saturdays were busy, but in the fall people seemed to come out of the woodwork to do their early Christmas shopping. Many of them also purchased Martha's home-baked goods—whoopie pies, cookies, muffins, banana nut bread, zucchini bread, lemon poppy seed bread, and so on. The cranberry bread loaves were particularly requested this autumn season. Still other customers found the antique oil lamps and kitchenware intriguing. A couple of ladies seemed interested in the secondhand books, many of which had a local Amish theme. It always brought a smile to Elizabeth's face to recommend local authors or to tell customers about the weekly quilt guild that met in the store.

With only ten minutes to spare before she had to leave for the auction, Elizabeth checked out a large wrought iron wall piece a woman had selected.

"Coming here is a bit like going on a scavenger hunt," the woman said as she fingered the beautiful piece. "You just never know what you're going to find."

"True." Elizabeth nodded. "Come back in a few days, and you'll see that we've added some things. I'm going to an auction today and should pick up a lot of new items." She paused to think through her choice of wording. "Well, not new. Just new-to-us."

"Oh, that's wonderful. I'll be back in a couple of days, then. Can't wait." The woman left with her new treasure, all smiles.

Elizabeth couldn't help but feel the strangest twist of emotions—her purchases at today's auction would help restock the shelves, but what a sad situation for the bishop's family.

Another glance at her watch told her it was time to leave. Elizabeth walked the aisles of the store until she finally located Martha, Mary, and Anna looking over an antique chandelier. They were deep in their conversation, and she hated to disturb them but had no choice.

Elizabeth cleared her throat. "Ladies, I hate to cut your meeting short, but Martha and I have got to get over to the Wittmers' place. The silent auction starts at three o'clock, and I want to be there in plenty of time to bid on lots of great items."

"Oh my." Martha's nose wrinkled as she glanced at her watch. "Is it really time to go?"

"Yes, sorry." Elizabeth turned her attention to Mary. "Are you still okay to stay here and mind the shop while we're gone?"

"Of course." With the wave of a hand Mary appeared to dismiss any concerns on that account.

And then there was Anna. Judging from the pout, she wasn't happy to be losing her cake baker. "It's just that Martha and I are still up to our eyeballs in cake talk," she said, her lips curling down into a frown. "Do you really have to steal her away from me right now, when I need her most?" She gave Elizabeth a pleading look.

Great. Looked like she would be going alone.

"I guess that's okay. If you ladies trust me to make the decisions on my own."

"Of course." Martha beamed. "You have such great taste, Elizabeth. We completely trust you."

"All right." Elizabeth walked to the front counter and retrieved her purse from the shelf underneath. She pulled out her car keys and headed to the door. Mary caught her just as she was leaving. "Thanks for doing this."

"It's no problem."

"If you happen to see anything that might work for Anna's wedding, go ahead and buy it, along with whatever else you think might sell. Think rustic."

"Will do." Elizabeth paused to think through her next words. "Though, between us, I think we need to be careful not to overdo things where Anna's concerned."

"Overdo?"

"You know what I mean. This is her wedding. She's footing the bill. I know you're trying to save her money by loaning her items from the store, but when we start buying new items with her in mind, then things could get tricky."

Crinkles formed between Mary's brows. "We can always sell them after the wedding."

"I know, but it seems like a lot of trouble to go through for someone else's wedding. And we can't guarantee that everything will sell. We've had some of these items since the store was open for business before we took over."

Mary placed her hand on Elizabeth's arm. Concern registered in her eyes. "Are you feeling left out of the wedding plans? Is that what this is about?"

"No. Not at all."

"Afraid we're going to overlook your birthday next week because we're so busy?"

Elizabeth was flabbergasted at such a comment. "Of course not. And for the record, I'm interested in Anna's wedding, of course. I'm very happy for her. I'm just anxious to get going to this auction so I'm not outbid."

"Okay, if you're sure that's all it is."

"It is. Now, I'd better get going."

A few minutes later Elizabeth turned her SUV onto Ronks Road. She slowed to a stop at the first corner and took in the breathtaking view. Off in the distance the usually green rolling fields were starting to show signs of seasonal changes. Gone were the vibrant green leaves in the trees. In their places, a colorful array of harvest colors beckoned.

She turned her SUV into the driveway at the Wittmer farm and searched for a place to park. Rows of buggies greeted her, along with a few vehicles. It looked like half of Bird-in-Hand had turned up for the auction.

Elizabeth got out of the car and pulled her purse strap over her shoulder. She walked past the throng of people, greeting a few friends along the way. Once she entered the barn, she saw the rows of items on display for the silent auction. Just what she'd come looking for.

"Welcome, Elizabeth." Susanna Wittmer extended her hand. "The auctioneer will get started at four o'clock. Until then, feel free to participate in the silent auction. All of the smaller items on the tables are ready for bidders. Just choose what you like."

"Thank you, Susanna." Elizabeth had her eye on a stack of cookbooks at this very moment. Those always sold well in the shop.

"We have a lot of items for sale. When *Maam* died years ago, we could not bear to let go of her things." Susanna's eyes flooded with tears. "But now that *Daed* has gone too, we are finally ready to say goodbye to some of their belongings. It is so hard though."

"How well I know." Elizabeth's thoughts flashed back to when her mother died and the many items they still hadn't given up. She patted Susanna's hand. "My prayers are with you. You will get through this, I promise."

"Thank you. I know we will." Susanna wiped her eyes with the back of her hand. "My husband has been such a big help. We have our own farm to manage, of course. My brothers are staying on here, but they have no need for most of these items. So we are letting go of what we can. It is difficult, but necessary."

"I understand."

Susanna turned her attention to another guest, and Elizabeth walked down the first aisle. She saw several items of interest, things that would be perfect for the shop. Glass canisters, baking items, even an old-fashioned meat grinder. She placed bids on all of them. Mary and Martha would be thrilled if she came back to the shop with these items in tow.

Elizabeth made a careful examination of every item she passed on the other aisles as well, pausing to bid on a cookie jar, a handmade wooden calendar, and several kerosene lamps. A set of cast-iron skillets caught her eye. They were always great sellers at the shop. But what really took her breath away were the Griswold baking molds. If she could get them for a good price, they would bring in a pretty penny.

On and on she went, bidding on linens, beautiful embroidery work, and multiple sets of crockery.

Just about the time she reached the end of the final aisle, Elizabeth discovered something that stopped her in her tracks—a porcelain washbasin in a familiar pattern. Very familiar.

"Whoa." She ran her finger over the interior of the bowl. Could it be?

This bowl was an exact match to the pitcher she'd purchased from the man at the shop.

CHAPTER THREE

W hat in the world?" Elizabeth reached down to touch the washbasin, astounded at her find. This was perfect.

She reached down to place her bid, but someone pressed into the spot right next to her and swept the porcelain basin off the table.

"Elizabeth, forgive me, but there has been a mistake." Susanna was wide-eyed and appeared upset about something.

"A mistake?"

"Yes." Susanna turned red in the face as she held tight to the washbasin in her arms. "My apologies if you were planning to bid on this. It is not for sale. I cannot believe my brother would put it out here. We agreed not to sell this one. It was Maam's favorite. It is an antique, very valuable. Worth far too much to let it go at auction. And it holds special significance to the family. I am sure you understand."

"Oh my goodness. Well, of course, but—"

"It means too much to ever sell."

"It is very lovely. And I was going to ask you about it anyway because I just happen to have—" Before she could finish her sentence, Susanna turned to speak to a customer who had a question about another item.

"Easy come, easy go." Elizabeth couldn't believe the turn of events. She was sad to lose the washbasin but needed to stay focused on the other items at the auction.

She took a few minutes to visit with friends then walked the aisles once more, upping her bids on items where she'd already been outbid by those coming along behind her. On her second go-round she happened to notice several framed chalkboards. These would be perfect for Anna's wedding to designate the various areas. Mary had such lovely handwriting. She could make these look really nice, and they would fit in with the rest of the decor.

Elizabeth placed a bid on the chalkboards. She continued to pace, her thoughts on the washbasin. The more she thought about it, the more she questioned the design. Maybe it wasn't a perfect match, anyway. A lot of these porcelain pieces looked similar, after all. Yes, surely she'd imagined the resemblance.

At ten minutes till four, Elizabeth decided to make one last round to make sure she hadn't been outbid on anything. Just as she reached the end of the second aisle she ran headlong into local police officer John Marks, who was talking to one of the Wittmer brothers.

John looked her way, and a smile tipped up the edges of his lips. He ran his fingers through his salt-and-pepper hair and took a step in her direction. "Hey, Elizabeth."

"Hey back. I'm sorry, I didn't mean to interrupt your conversation."

"No interruption at all. James was just telling me that they'll be announcing the winners of the silent auction in ten minutes. Then the auctioneer will get the ball rolling on the big stuff."

"Good. I've already placed bids on quite a few things for the shop." She paused and gazed into his intense blue eyes. "I'm glad you're here, actually. Let me get your take on what you think I should do." Elizabeth filled him in, first telling him about the pitcher she'd purchased from the man at the shop, and then about the basin she'd just seen.

"I'm worried that it might be the same design," she confessed.

"I suppose it's possible. Or maybe the two items are completely unrelated," John said. "Are you sure it wasn't the same? Those pitcher and basin sets are a dime a dozen around here. I see them in every shop."

"Right, but Susanna told me the basin is an antique, very valuable. If they're similar in design, then maybe the pitcher is valuable too."

"Maybe you could check out the logo and then do some research."

"I'll do that. I didn't offer much money to the man who sold me the pitcher. Just thirty dollars. I'm feeling bad about that, if it's as valuable as Susanna's basin. Sounds like I really do need to do a little research on the brand name and then reach out to him." She paused. "But first I have to find him."

"You didn't get his information?"

"No. He didn't place the pitcher on consignment. I purchased it outright, so I never thought to get his information. Dumb move, I guess."

"Not dumb at all." John gave her a sympathetic look. "You didn't realize there was more to the story."

"Looks like I've got a bit of sleuthing to do." She glanced over at the chalkboards and realized someone else was placing a bid on them. "But first, to secure these bids." Elizabeth took off, determined not to be outdone.

R-r-ring!

Martha reached for her cell phone and noticed Elizabeth's name on the incoming call. She turned to face the bride-to-be. "I'm so sorry, Anna, but I have to take this. It's Elizabeth, calling from the auction."

From the looks of things, Anna didn't even seem to notice. She was busy scrolling through wedding cake photos on her phone.

Martha answered the call with a quick "Hello?"

"Martha, have you got a minute?" From the other end of the line, Elizabeth sounded anxious.

Martha glanced at Anna, who continued to ramble on about cake toppers, baby's breath, and hydrangeas.

"Sure. What's up?"

"Well, I'm still out at the Wittmer place."

"Hopefully finding lots of great things."

"Yes, I managed to snag twenty or twenty-five items that will be perfect for the store, but that's not why I'm calling. I'm wondering if you can do me a favor."

"Okay." Martha shifted the phone to her other ear.

"You know that beautiful cream and rose pitcher I bought a few days back? I think it's on the housewares aisle, second shelf from the top near the back of the store."

"Sure, I remember."

"Two things." Elizabeth sounded a little out of breath. "First, pull it off the shelf and put it in the stockroom."

"You don't want to sell it?"

"I'm not sure it's really ours to sell."

This made no sense at all. "But you paid cash for it, right? So of course it's ours. We can do what we like with it."

"Right. I know we paid for it, but I'm not sure the man who sold it to me knew its true value. I don't think I gave him a fair price. I'm going to research the brand a little further and let you know what I find out."

Martha couldn't help but gasp. "Really? You think it's worth a lot of money?"

Anna looked up from her phone, worry lines on her forehead. "Has something gone wrong?"

"No." Martha shook her head. "Everything's fine. I'll be done in a minute."

"Wait, is that Anna?" Elizabeth's words sounded more curt than usual. "She's still there? Does she know we've got a business to run?"

"Mary is manning the register, Elizabeth. Deep breath." Martha tried to keep her now-lowered voice on an even keel. "Now, tell me again why I'm putting this pitcher in the back of the shop. You think it's an antique?"

"I don't know. I would like to compare the logos, but I don't think this is the best time to talk to Susanna. She seems pretty overwhelmed. But just in case, I'd like to pull it. And when you get it to the back of the store, would you mind taking a picture of it and texting it to me? I need to solidify something in my mind. I just need to see if the design matches a washbasin I found here. Oh, and take a picture of the logo too. It wasn't a familiar name. I'd like to look it up."

"Oh. Okay. I'll get right on it." Martha ended the call. Moments later, she located the pitcher in question. She had just turned back toward the front of the shop when the front doorbell sounded.

An unfamiliar couple entered, dressed to the nines. The woman's makeup was impeccable, and her designer purse matched her ensemble. Probably tourists. Folks around here didn't really make such a fuss. Just about the time Mary called out a welcome from her spot at the cash register, a dog bounded between the couple, nearly knocking the poor fellow over. The dog headed straight toward Martha. She clutched the pitcher as tightly as she could.

"What in the world?" Martha barely caught a glimpse of the pooch as he raced past her toward the back of the store. "Where did he come from?" Before she could gather her wits about her, the dog started barking.

From the back of the store, Anna called out a "Whoa, Nellie!" and then let out a shriek as a loud crash sounded.

Martha took off running, still clutching the pitcher. She felt her breath catch in her throat as she saw Anna on the floor of the stockroom with the dog on top of her.

"Are you okay?" Martha asked.

Anna nodded as the dog licked her face. "I…well, I was. Before this monster attacked me."

"He attacked you?" These words came from Mary, who must have heard all the commotion from the front of the store. She now stood beside Martha, worry lines etched into her forehead.

"Not technically." Anna tried to push the dog off of her, but he refused to budge. "I think maybe he's just overly affectionate. But it caused a moment of panic on my part. I didn't see him coming."

Martha gave the dog a closer look and realized it was the same boxer she'd seen before, just a few days back. With the man who'd sold them the pitcher—the same pitcher she now held in her hands.

She clutched it a bit tighter, more perplexed by the timing of the dog's appearance than anything.

"He sure is a sweet thing." Mary leaned over and scratched him behind the ears.

"Sweet?" Anna scrambled to stand. "Are we forgetting that he knocked me down?"

Martha set the pitcher on the table and then turned back to deal with Anna and the dog.

A crowd had gathered at the stockroom door way. The woman the dog had nearly bowled over upon entering the store was now scratching the pup's head. "You're a handsome little man," she cooed. She looked up at the ladies. "You've got a great watchdog here, ladies. Boxers are the best."

"Oh, he's not ours," Martha responded. And she would hardly call the dog little. He had to be sixty pounds, if not more.

The woman turned her attention to one of the quilts on the far wall, and the dog took a couple of steps toward Anna.

The terrified bride-to-be clutched her scrapbook and took a giant step backward. "Keep that animal away from me, Martha. He's already plowed me down once. I don't need to end up with a broken leg a week before my wedding."

"Come here, pup." Martha clucked her tongue and hoped the dog would obey.

The dog let out a pitiful whimper and rubbed his head against her leg.

"Do you think he's in pain?" Mary asked. "It seems like he's trying to tell us something."

"Let me look him over. Maybe he's injured, and we just can't see it." Martha knelt down next to the pup and ran her hands over his torso and then each of his legs. Nothing seemed out of the ordinary. "I don't feel any obvious injuries, and he didn't flinch, so I really don't know what to think."

"I think we should call animal control. That's what I think." Anna folded her arms across her chest.

The dog let out another whimper. "There, there, boy." Martha searched her memory bank to come up with a name. "You're going to be okay."

"Do we have a record of where his owner lives?" Mary asked.

"I don't think so. Elizabeth didn't buy the pitcher on consignment, as I recall. But I do remember her saying something that day about the man's red truck." She paused. "This whole thing is so strange. Elizabeth just called about that very pitcher. She thinks there's a bigger story behind it, that maybe it's worth a lot of money or something like that."

"Whoa." Mary's eyes widened.

"Right. Sounded like a long story. But the point is, she's looking for the man who brought the pitcher in. He happens to be the owner of this dog." She glanced down to check for a collar, but the dog wasn't wearing one. Now what?

"Oh, I know!" Mary snapped her fingers as an idea hit. "We could take him to the vet's office and see if he's microchipped. They'll know what to do from there."

"Perfect." Martha glanced at Anna. "Do you mind? We were almost done, anyway."

"Were we?" Anna didn't look convinced. "I guess I could send you the rest of the cake pictures when I get back to the house. I'm pretty sure I've narrowed it down to the five-tiered one with the black piping. But I'll let you know."

Martha fought the temptation to groan aloud. She could only imagine the amount of effort such a cake would require.

Anna tucked her phone into her purse and pressed the scrapbook under her arm. "Guess I'll see you tomorrow, ladies. Thanks for your help with everything. I can't wait to see what Elizabeth brings back from the auction." She headed toward the front door, still rambling on and on about the wedding decor.

Before anyone could stop him, the hyperactive boxer took off after her. He bounded through the open door and into the parking lot.

"Oh no!" Martha sprinted after him but couldn't catch up. By the time she reached the edge of the parking lot, the dog had disappeared from view.

She paused to catch her breath just as Mary caught up with her.

"I hope he doesn't get hit by a car."

"He made it here. Surely he'll make it back home again."

"Wherever *home* is." Mary turned back toward the store. "Guess we'll never know now."

"Right." Martha toyed with the idea of getting in her car and following the dog down the highway to see where he landed. Just as she gave the idea more thought, she realized something important.

She still needed to take a snapshot of the pitcher for Elizabeth.

CHAPTER FOUR

During the Sunday morning service at Mount Zion Mennonite Church, Pastor Nagle preached on new life in Christ. Elizabeth tried to stay focused, especially during the closing hymn, one of her favorites. But her thoughts kept drifting back to the pitcher and washbasin and to the owner of the dog Rocky.

After church, the sisters enjoyed a tasty lunch at a local smorgasbord. When they arrived home, Elizabeth changed into comfortable clothing and settled into a chair on the front porch with a book. Pal, their border collie, curled up at her feet, content to rest for a while.

She couldn't help but smile as she listened to Reddy—the farm's token rooster—fussing in the distance. His voice merged with the high-pitched bleats coming from Wynken, Blynken, and Nod, the pygmy goats.

"We've got quite the menagerie here, Pal," Elizabeth said as she leaned back against the chair.

Not that she would change a thing. The comfortable sounds of the farm made her feel right at home.

Mary came out of the house with Tink, their dachshund, tagging along. She took a seat next to Elizabeth and stared out over their property. "It won't be long before we'll be stuck indoors." She tugged at her sweater and shivered. "Winter will be here sooner than we know. It seems like the seasons are just buzzing by."

"True. I'd like to squeeze out every minute of autumn I can," Elizabeth responded. "It's my favorite season but seems far too short."

"Agreed. I love everything about it—the colors, the scents, the harvest...everything!"

"Me too." At her feet, Butterscotch, their cat, began to purr. She wound herself around Elizabeth's ankles, begging for attention. "All right, all right." She reached down and gave the kitty what he was yearning for, a scratch behind the ears.

"You've unleashed a monster," Mary warned. "Once you start that, he won't want you to stop."

"I know, but he won't leave me alone until I give him a little attention." After a moment, Elizabeth paused and looked around. "Where's Martha? Why isn't she out here resting? It's Sunday."

"She's baking, of course." Mary laughed. "You know how she is. She doesn't consider it work. To her, it's therapy. She might even argue that it's an act of worship."

"I understand." Elizabeth gave the cat one last pat on the head then shooed him away. "Not that baking is therapy for me, but I can understand how it could be...for Martha."

"I'm just relieved Martha's past that coffee cake kick she was on. I mean, I love a good coffee cake, but even I have my limits."

"Me too. So what's she baking up in there today?"

"Snickerdoodles. I tried to grab a warm one from the cooling rack, and she slapped my hand. She said, 'Touch that, and

I'll snicker your doodle!'" Mary laughed. "I told her she sounded like Mama."

"Mama and her expressions. How I loved them." Elizabeth lost herself to bittersweet memories for a moment.

"Remember that old phrase she used to use: 'I'm moving slower than a Sunday afternoon!'" Mary leaned back against the chair and sighed. "That's me. Today."

"Me too. Mama had it right."

The two sisters settled into a comfortable silence— Elizabeth with her book and Mary gazing off in the distance at the beautiful fall leaves. Butterscotch continued to meow until he realized Elizabeth wasn't going to offer any more scratches. Then he curled up on the porch next to Tink.

Sometime around three o'clock, one of their neighbors, Rachel Fischer, stopped by for a visit. Martha took a break from her baking and joined them on the porch, where they discussed the goings-on in their community. Elizabeth broached the subject of the Wittmers with caution.

"How do you feel the auction went?" she asked.

Rachel shrugged. "I am not sure they got the prices they were hoping for on the larger items, but—in part, thanks to you—the silent auction went well. Thank you for placing so many bids. It meant a lot to them."

"We needed the merchandise." Elizabeth yawned and leaned back in her chair. "It's going to be nice to place so many new things on our shelves, that's for sure. There's nothing I love more than filling our shelves with new-to-us items to sell."

"But I do understand how hard it must have been for the Wittmers to get rid of their parents' things," Mary was quick to add. "We haven't even tried to go through Mama's things yet."

"It'll come, in time," Elizabeth said. "We'll get there."

"Hopefully sooner rather than later," Martha said from the doorway, in her usual matter-of-fact way. "At some point you just have to be objective. It's just stuff, after all."

"But some of that 'stuff' has memories attached," Elizabeth countered. "Which is what makes it so hard." In fact, some of Mama's items would be impossible to let go of…ever.

Rachel patted her on the arm. "True, true. But your mama loved this shop and would want it to thrive. No doubt she would be happy to have those items on the shelves instead of tucked away in an attic or closet somewhere."

For the life of her, Elizabeth couldn't find a counterargument to that point.

Elizabeth thought about Rachel's words for the rest of the day. She and her sisters would eventually need to go through Mama's things. That was inevitable. But right now she simply couldn't convince herself of that fact. The memories attached to the items were still too fresh, too powerful. How the Wittmers could have let go of their parents' belongings so quickly was a mystery to her. Then again, the Amish didn't place much stock in worldly goods. Perhaps they had the right perspective about all of that. Maybe those items were—as Martha said—just "stuff."

When she fell asleep that night, she dreamed about Mama's sewing machine. In the dream she was a little girl, watching her mother stitch together a dress—a gingham dress meant for school. Mama turned and held the dress up with a smile.

"It'll be the perfect fit for you, Elizabeth. What do you think?"

"Perfect, Mama!" She reached to grab it, all smiles, but the dress disappeared before her eyes, ghosted away...just like Mama.

Elizabeth awoke with the memories of her mother fresh on her mind. She pressed away the heaviness in her heart as she prepared for her day. There was no time to get emotional today, not with so much to be done. She dressed in her favorite blue blouse and black slacks then chose her most comfortable shoes.

After a quick breakfast, she and her sisters headed to the shop, where they turned their attention to sorting through Elizabeth's purchases from the silent auction. They priced each one and put it on display, except for the items Mary felt might be useful for the wedding.

The shop didn't have much business in the first hour or two, so Elizabeth decided to spend the time learning more about the pitcher. If it was truly valuable, she would try to track down the man who'd sold it to her. Why, oh why, hadn't she taken his information? Oh well. She would do her best to locate that red Ford truck, the one with the American flag bumper sticker with the words SEMPER FI above it. If she could find the truck, she could find the owner.

She got caught up in research about the pitcher, and time flew by. The shop really filled up around lunchtime. As was often the case, folks headed over to Martha's bakery case to purchase sweet treats.

Sometime around one thirty the crowd thinned, and the sisters gathered together at the register to talk.

Elizabeth set the pitcher down on the countertop, using great care. After what she'd just learned, she needed to treat it with kid gloves.

"Well?" Martha leaned against the counter and gazed at the pitcher. "What have you learned?"

"I've done a lot more research on the maker of the pitcher," Elizabeth explained. "It's a china company in the UK called Foley Wileman."

"Wow." Martha gave the pitcher an admiring gaze. "This came all the way from England?"

"Yes, and probably close to one hundred and fifty years ago."

"Whoa." Martha leaned back, as if afraid to touch it. "Are you sure, Elizabeth?"

She nodded. "From the best I can figure, yes. I kept checking and double-checking. There are pieces like this at auction houses, going for big bucks. And there are a few being auctioned on eBay as well, but some of them are damaged. This one is in perfect condition."

Mary's eyes widened. "So why would a man bring something this valuable to a secondhand shop and not sell it on eBay or at an auction? Makes no sense at all."

"Either he didn't realize its worth," Elizabeth said, "or he wanted to get rid of it quickly without leaving a paper trail. We have to consider both options. And right now I'm torn between the two. I've been kicking myself that I didn't take the piece on consignment. Then I'd have his contact information."

"The plot thickens." Mary picked up the pitcher, turned it over, and read the stamp on the bottom.

"Careful!" Elizabeth put her hands up in the air, terrified her sister might accidentally drop it.

Mary put it back down and backed away from it. "Okay, okay. I was just checking to make sure you'd read the name right."

"I did." Elizabeth sighed.

"What do we know about this man, anyway?" Martha reached for a pen and paper. She seemed ready to jot down any notes. "Was there anything about him that stood out to you?"

Elizabeth stopped to think through the events of his visit to the store. "Nothing terribly consequential. But I did find it odd that he looked so frail. At first I thought he was an older man, but when he got close I could see that he was probably only in his late thirties. He was already wrinkled and had a bit of gray in his hair."

"I had a friend in Indianapolis who went completely gray over a period of a few months," Mary said. "He was only thirty-five at the time, which is why I remember it so vividly. He went through a family tragedy. His son died in a terrible accident, and he aged immediately. It was difficult to watch."

"Yes, it happens," Martha agreed. "I've seen people age overnight after traumas."

"I really don't know how old this man was, for sure," Elizabeth said. "But there were other things that stood out about him. His clothes were a little ragged. I do remember that. He looked a little...down on his luck. What was that phrase Mama used to use? 'Too poor to paint, too proud to whitewash.'"

"I haven't heard that one in years." Mary laughed. "Mama and her sayings."

"She had one for every occasion," Martha said. "Remember when I would act up, and she would ask if my knickers were in a knot?"

This got a laugh out of everyone.

Just as quickly, Mary's smile tilted downward into a frown. "But if that man was really down on his luck, it would explain what he was doing selling off his possessions. Maybe he needed the money."

"I feel bad that we didn't give him what it was worth," Martha was quick to add. "Especially if he is really down on his luck. If it's valuable, he needs to know. That money could mean a lot to him."

"Right." Elizabeth paced back and forth, deep in thought. She paused and stared at the pitcher. "Not that we're in a position to pay what a pitcher like that is really worth. He needs to take it to someone who deals with true antiques. And here's a question for you. Do either of you find it odd that a man would bring in an item like a porcelain pitcher in the first place? It's pretty girlie, no less—ivory with rose-colored flowers. Not exactly something a man would have used personally. And for sure he wasn't Amish. His clothes and truck were proof of that."

"You find that suspicious?" Mary asked.

"Not sure." Elizabeth shrugged. "I'm just saying, it's usually women who bring in housewares, especially the pretty things like those pitchers and washbasins. Men bring in yard equipment and tools, stuff like that."

"Remember that time Mr. Biederman brought in that porcelain doll?" Martha asked. "It belonged to his daughter, the one who left home and refused to speak to him. He told me it was easier to let go of it than to look at it, because the memories were too painful. So he chose to sell it to spare himself the heartache whenever he looked at it."

"Sad," Elizabeth said.

"Yes. So I guess we have to conclude that we'll have men come through with 'girlie' items from time to time."

"I guess." Elizabeth gave her thoughts over to the seller of the pitcher once more. He seemed like a nice enough man, nothing outwardly suspicious about him. And he wasn't the one requesting a cash purchase, was he? He might have been just fine with putting the pitcher on consignment. That whole cash deal had been her idea, hadn't it?

Martha pursed her lips as she lifted the pitcher for a closer look. "This is one of the risks of having a secondhand store, I guess. We're liable to underpay on true valuables from time to time."

"Right." Elizabeth nodded. "I'll give Susanna a call to ask for more information about her set. She might know more about the worth of the pitcher we bought. I'm still not one hundred percent sure the pattern is identical, though it seems like a close match to me. I sure wish I'd taken a picture or seen the label on the bottom of hers. Maybe she'll let me give it a closer look."

"Well, of course," Martha responded. "If it's really an antique, it's worth a fortune. So that's likely why she was so worked up about her brothers putting it out to sell. I'd be upset at them too. I say we ask about it, even if it opens a scab of some sort."

"Agreed. I'll call her right away, then." Elizabeth entered Susanna's number into her phone. It rang three times and then went to voice mail. She'd expected as much, since the Wittmers' phone was in a shack at the end of their driveway. She had no choice but to leave a message.

"Susanna, this is Elizabeth Classen." She cleared her throat. "I wanted to ask you some questions about that antique washbasin I saw at the auction. We purchased a similar piece, and I'm trying to estimate its value. I thought perhaps you could help. Just give me a call when you can."

When she ended the call, Elizabeth said, "I feel like I need to return this pitcher to the man."

"Good idea," Mary said. "I agree. Then he can sell it to someone better qualified to give him what it's worth."

Elizabeth nodded. "Right. I say we track down his vehicle. There's got to be some way to find out who owns a red Ford F-150 in Lancaster County."

"Probably hundreds of people," Mary said.

"Maybe." But Elizabeth wouldn't get discouraged. Not yet. "I'm guessing it was only four or five years old. I say we enter the type of vehicle into the computer's search engine along with the words *Lancaster County* to see if anything comes up." She opened her laptop and went to her search engine, where she began to browse. "I see a lot of red trucks. Most are vehicles for sale, though. He wouldn't be selling his truck."

"That we know of," Mary countered.

"Right. Good point. Well, I guess I'll just follow the trail of any red truck in Lancaster County."

As Elizabeth browsed the internet on her laptop she did her best to remember the details of that day. The weary-looking man with the plaid shirt. His golden tan. The package in his arms. The beautiful pitcher. His handsome—albeit chaotic— boxer named Rocky. An American flag bumper sticker, along with the words SEMPER FI.

Elizabeth continued her online search for the truck. For a couple of minutes the room was quiet. After a moment, she gasped as a photo came into view. "Oh my goodness! Look at this. It's a Craigslist ad for a red truck matching the description of the one I saw!"

CHAPTER FIVE

Elizabeth stared at the photo, dumbfounded. She couldn't believe their good fortune. "This *has* to be it."

"Not necessarily." Martha pulled the laptop in her direction to give the picture a closer look. "There are probably dozens of red Ford trucks in our area. But it could be a lead."

"One worth checking out, right?" Elizabeth shifted the laptop back in her direction and looked over the ad with a closer eye. "There's a number for the seller right here. I say we call him and ask about the vehicle. Worst-case scenario, we've got the wrong guy." She reached for the phone and punched in the number.

A few seconds later, a very rushed voice greeted her. "Truck's already sold."

Okay then.

They kept browsing until Mary happened upon another possibility.

"This one's in Perkasie, so quite a distance away, but anything's possible, right?"

Elizabeth called the number. After a couple of rings, an elderly woman answered the call. As it turned out the truck was really a Chevy, not a Ford. There had been a misprint in the ad. Oh well. Maybe this whole venture was ill-fated. Maybe she didn't need to be putting her nose in a stranger's business.

They were just about to give up altogether when Mary happened to stumble across an advertisement for a used-car dealership in Lancaster. There, plain as day, was a photo of a truck that looked exactly like the F-150 driven by the man with the dog.

Elizabeth punched in the number and prayed for a positive outcome.

"Chester's Autos." The voice on the other end of the line sounded irritated. "This is Chester. How can I help you?"

"Yes, hello. I'm calling about a red Ford F-150 you've got listed. Do you still have it available?"

"Sure do." The fellow kicked into super-salesman gear, his voice now slick and polished. "Mighty glad you asked. It's an XLT, rear-wheel drive, automatic electronic eco boost. Anything else you want to know?"

"Oh, well I—"

"V6, so plenty of pickup." He chuckled. "Get it? *Pickup?* Pretty funny, huh? Sometimes I even make myself laugh."

"Right. Funny. But—"

"Twin turbocharged ABS brakes, illuminated entry, remote keyless entry. What do you think? Sound like what you're looking for?"

"Well, I'm glad you asked, because I just wanted to ask you—"

"Oh, I forgot to mention the traction control. That's important. And it's low on miles, which is pretty amazing for an F-150. They're great work trucks."

"Of course—"

"But it's getting a lot of interest, so if you want to see it, you'd better come quick. I guarantee you this one won't be on the lot for long. Folks around here snatch up these trucks in no time."

For a moment it sounded like the fellow might hang up, so Elizabeth interjected a quick question. "Did you acquire the truck recently, then?"

"Yep." He started talking to someone else, and she seemed to have lost him for a minute.

"Do you mind if I ask when?" Elizabeth asked when he finally paused for air from his other conversation.

"Got it a couple of days back. Saturday, to be precise. And she's a real beaut. The owner took excellent care of it. Just 37,000 miles and the body's in great shape. I think you're really gonna love the features, like I said. It's easy to handle on the road and great on back roads too." He returned to his other conversation, as if forgetting she was still on the line.

"Did this truck, by any chance, have a Semper Fi bumper sticker on the back of it?"

"Hmm." The man paused. "Don't remember that. But you're welcome to come down and give it a look. I don't think you'll be able to walk away once you've laid eyes on it. She can be yours for just $18,999. That's a real steal for a truck that's only four years old."

"Right."

"And you can't beat Ford for dependability and mileage."

"Are you sure you're not related to my father?" Elizabeth asked, and then laughed.

"I suppose anything's possible. And I'll make you a deal... if you buy the truck, I'll track down a Semper Fi bumper sticker to put on it. I'm always happy to support the men and women

who serve our fine country." The man started talking to someone in the background again. When he returned, his words
sounded rushed. "Look, I'm really busy on this end, so I've
gotta go. I have another customer. But come on in as quick as
you can if you're really interested in seeing this vehicle. Otherwise you'll miss it, I guarantee. Oh, and bring your trade-in. I'll
give you a good deal on it, one you can't pass up."

"Oh, but I—"

He disappeared on her again.

Elizabeth ended the call and faced her sisters. "I need to
find out if that truck has a Semper Fi bumper sticker on it."

"Right. So which of us is going to watch the store while the
others leave?" Mary asked.

This took Elizabeth by surprise. "You don't think we should
wait until the end of the day? I'm pretty sure they'll still be
open. No point in tearing out of here on a whim when we don't
even know if we've got the right vehicle."

"What if he sells the truck to the person who just came
into his office?" Mary argued. "Then what? Besides, business has been slow today. I'm sure one person can manage
alone."

"True. I see your point."

"Elizabeth is the one who talked to the man," Martha said.
"And she's the one who saw the truck firsthand. So she has to
go. That's the only thing that makes sense." She nodded at an
incoming customer and then lowered her voice. "I'll stay here
and watch the shop if you want to go with her, Mary."

"Sure, I'll go along for the ride." Mary shrugged and
brushed some crumbs off the countertop. "If you're sure."

"I'm sure. Just don't be gone too long. Oh, and pick up some baking powder while you're out, if you don't mind. I need it for the biscuits I'm making tomorrow morning. Otherwise I'll have to come up with a new plan."

"If we have time," Mary responded. "I don't have any idea how long all of this is going to take."

"Hopefully not too long," Elizabeth said.

As she led the way out to her SUV, her hands were trembling. This whole thing had her a little unnerved. What was the point of getting involved in all of this, anyway? Oh yes, to locate the man who'd sold her the expensive pitcher. To make sure he knew the pitcher was valuable. To make sure his dog made it home okay.

Mary must have noticed her reticence. "You want me to drive so you can focus on the directions? I'm clueless about where this place is, and one of us will have to keep an eye on her phone so we don't get lost."

"Sure." Elizabeth handed her the keys. "I just know it's called Chester's Autos."

"That's a memorable name." Mary laughed. "Just look it up on your phone, and we'll go from there."

Elizabeth got into the passenger seat and pulled up the dealership on her phone. "Looks like it's off 222. Shouldn't take us too long to get there."

"Got it." Mary slid behind the wheel and turned on the car. She switched the radio to a different station than Elizabeth usually listened to. Seconds later, a familiar oldie from the fifties filled the space between them.

When they passed the Wittmer farm, Elizabeth noticed several buggies lined up in the driveway. Her mind shifted back to the silent auction and that beautiful porcelain washbasin, how Susanna had snatched it from her before she could ask about it. How mortified she must have been that her brothers were willing to sell it off.

Not that it was any of Elizabeth's business, of course.

"Looks like folks are still coming out in force to support the family. Just one more thing to love about the Amish community. They take care of their own."

"Hmm?" Elizabeth snapped to attention. "Oh, right. I don't know how people survive without folks around to support them. When Mama died, we were surrounded on every side by caring people who went out of their way to make us feel loved. But I know it's not always like that. Some people have no support system whatsoever. I don't know how they manage in a crisis. I really don't."

"Me neither."

Elizabeth waved at Frankie Wittmer as they drove by. He tipped his hat and offered a broad smile. Then he turned back to his brother George. Elizabeth couldn't help but wonder what they were talking about. Were they missing their father? Were they trying to make decisions about the farm? She remembered all too clearly the things her family discussed in the days and weeks after Mama's death. So many details needed tending to, and she'd been the one to see to many of them. As her mother's caregiver, it just made sense. But there were days when it all felt completely overwhelming.

"You okay over there?" Mary's voice startled her back to reality once more.

"Oh, yes. Sure."

Mary tapped the brakes as they drew up to a stop sign. Elizabeth waved at an Amish woman who was raking leaves near the edge of the road. Autumn was in full swing in Lancaster County. The brisk weather made for lovely days outdoors, albeit a bit chilly as of late. But nothing could beat the harvest season.

"Did you hear that Rachel's family is doing the corn maze again this year?" Mary asked.

"Yes. She invited me to walk the orchards with her too. When things slow down, I plan to do just that."

"Martha will be thrilled if we show up with fruit for pies." Mary sighed. "I just love this time of year. Local produce. Fruit and vegetable stands. Farmers markets. Everything that's good about the Amish country, all rolled into one glorious season."

"I agree," Elizabeth said.

"Good! Then maybe I can talk you into a hot-air balloon ride this year." Mary lifted a brow. "'Tis the season."

"Um, no thank you." Elizabeth laughed and settled back against her seat and enjoyed the view as her sister picked up speed. "I'm not that adventurous, sorry."

Moments later, they were headed toward the highway. Mary sang an old fifties song at the top of her lungs. Elizabeth wondered what it would be like to have a heart filled with such merriment. Her sister was so adventurous, getting a thrill out of things like hot-air balloon rides and corn mazes. In fact, the hot-pink top she was wearing matched her attitude toward life—cheerful and bright. Oh, to be so free and easy, so fun to be around. And generous as well. That's why Mary cared so much about Anna's wedding, not to impress others with her creativity, but to be a help to a friend.

Of course, that generosity had gotten her in trouble a time or two, especially when it came to her ex-husband, Brian. That scoundrel had taken advantage of Mary's generous nature more times than any of them would like to count.

These days, Mary was navigating the waters of single-ness just like her sisters. And though she'd only been back in Bird-in-Hand a few months, she seemed to be doing well.

"Hey, which way should we go?" Mary's words startled Elizabeth back to attention. "Should we take 30 or stay on 340 the whole way?"

"I'd say to stay on 340. It's quicker and intersects with 222." Elizabeth glanced down at her phone. "Sorry. I totally forgot I was supposed to be navigating."

"That's okay. Things haven't changed too much over the years. I could probably find it if I had to."

They drove past Bird-in-Hand's Farmers Market, and Elizabeth fought the temptation to ask Mary to stop for a few minutes so she could shop. The market was one of her favorite places, especially in the fall. There she could find all sorts of fruits and tasty homemade items like jams and jellies. Of course, there were also vegetables in abundance, especially during harvest season. One could find them in colorful array— everything from deep purple eggplant to bright orange pump-kins to ruby red beets. But what really won her over were the meats, cheeses, and nuts. *Mmm.* She could almost taste them now.

"Did I lose you again?" Mary asked.

"Hmm?" Elizabeth laughed as she looked her sister's way. "No, just thinking about food. I can't drive past the Farmers Market without wanting to go inside."

Mary nodded. "I agree. And I've been thinking…that's the same sort of draw we want our store to have."

"I think I'm just drawn to good food," Elizabeth admitted.

"Aren't we all?" Mary laughed.

They spent the next several minutes talking about various ways they could bring more customers to their shop. Before long, they had arrived in Lancaster. Mary pulled up to Chester's Autos on 222, and their conversation about Secondhand Blessings ceased.

Elizabeth examined the car lot and its vast array of vehicles. Overhead, a multicolored vintage pennant banner framed out the area, its triangular flags waving in the afternoon breeze. At the entrance, a flashing neon sign proclaimed the best deals in town. And, as if that wasn't enough, a teenage boy in a cheetah costume directed them onto the lot with a crazy, over-the-top dance routine.

"Wow." Just one word from Mary summed up her take on the place.

Elizabeth couldn't help but agree. "Wow is right. I can't believe I haven't noticed this place before. It's bound to leave a lasting impression."

"Didn't it used to be Affordable Autos? At least, that's my recollection. I remember the TV commercials."

"Yes, I think you're right." Elizabeth gave the lot a closer look as they found a parking place. "Man, he's got a lot of cars. Kind of surprising for such a small place. And lots of customers too." The lot was teeming with people who meandered from vehicle to vehicle.

"Let's see what we can see. But just so you know in advance, if that cheetah heads our way, I'm out of here." Mary eased the car into a parking space and slid it into PARK. They got out and walked down the first row of cars. Just as a salesman in a seersucker suit approached them, Elizabeth spotted a red truck in the distance.

"Mary, look!" She barreled right past the salesman and didn't stop until the back bumper came into view. Sure enough, the words SEMPER FI above an American flag greeted her. Elizabeth could hardly contain her zeal as she exclaimed, "This is it!"

CHAPTER SIX

This is it?" The salesman approached Elizabeth, a wide smile on his face. He adjusted the collar of his seersucker suit. "Well, it doesn't take you long to pick out a vehicle, now does it? I'm glad you found what you were looking for. Here at Chester's Autos we aim to please."

"Oh, I—" Oops.

"Are you sure you don't even want to test drive her first before signing on the dotted line?" His bushy eyebrows arched in animated style. "I think you'll find she's in terrific condition. And I just had my mechanic run a check on the engine. Everything's in working order."

The salesman went into a spiel about the vehicle but lost Elizabeth a couple of sentences in. She walked around the truck and checked it over thoroughly. This was it. Mud flaps. Same American flag sticker below the SEMPER FI. This truck had belonged to the man who had sold them the pitcher.

The salesman paused for breath. "I'm glad you came when you did. I've had a lot of interest in this vehicle. Just had a call about it, in fact." He extended his hand. "Name's Chester O'Conner. I'm the owner."

"Elizabeth Classen. I called you earlier." She gave him a once-over as she shook his hand. The guy looked familiar, right down to the odd suit…but why? Oh yes. She remembered now.

He did that crazy, over-the-top commercial, the one where he spoke so fast she could barely make out what he was saying. Those commercials always annoyed her.

Chester wagged his index finger in her direction. "Oh, so *you're* the lady who was looking for this truck, then, are you? You didn't waste any time. Good for you, going after what you want. There's nothing finer than a customer who knows what he or she likes. Wish more folks were like that."

"Yes, well, I—"

"Just so you're aware..." Chester rested his hand on the hood. "I bought this truck from an elderly lady who only drove it to church on Sundays."

"You can skip all that," Mary said with the wave of a hand. "We've met the owner. He's no lady."

The salesman's face fell. "You know Jackson? Why didn't you just say so?"

Jackson. They had a name.

"You didn't give me much of a chance," Elizabeth reminded him. "He was a customer at our shop. I bought a porcelain pitcher from him last week. We've been trying to track him down."

"Must've been some pitcher."

"Well, we have more than one reason to track him down." Mary put her hand over her eyes to shield them from the sun. "His dog showed up at the shop yesterday and looked a bit... lost. We want to make sure he made it back home okay."

Chester's jaw dropped. "You saw Rocky?"

"You know the dog?" Elizabeth could hardly believe it.

Chester leaned his elbow against the truck. "Sure. Jackson came by three or four times over the past month, trying to decide if he should sell or not. I finally gave him an offer he couldn't refuse." Chester's face contorted. "Look, the truth is, I couldn't offer much. I knew he was down on his luck and needed the money, but I can only go so far in cutting a deal, even on a great truck like this. I'm sure you understand. I gotta do what I gotta do to stay in business."

"Of course."

"Rocky was with him every time he came by, including Saturday." Now Chester looked genuinely concerned. "Are you sure it was the same dog that showed up at your place?"

"Yes." Elizabeth was sure.

"No doubt about it," Mary added. "He turned up out of the blue on Saturday afternoon, without his owner, then he disappeared just as quickly. It was all so strange. So we've been on a quest to find his owner to make sure Rocky made it home. He wasn't wearing a collar the last time we saw him, and I have no idea if he's microchipped."

Chester shook his head. "Considering Jackson's current condition, I'd say probably not."

"What is his current condition, if you don't mind my asking?" Mary asked.

Chester's gaze shifted to the ground and then back up again. "Well, I don't really know the specifics, just that he's lost his job and been through a rough patch with family matters. I didn't feel like pressing him for more details. It's not my business to butt in."

"Of course. We're worried too. That's all." Elizabeth didn't feel she should say more.

Chester raked his fingers through his carefully combed hair, which left it in a messy state. "Okay, ladies...now you've got me worried. I was already a little concerned because Jackson didn't look great on the day I bought the truck. I do have his address. It's on the paperwork." His face grew stern. "Not that I can share that information with you, of course." His expression softened. "But I'll swing by his place and check on him after work. How would that be?"

"That would be great. And you'll call us? We'd like to get in touch with him on a matter that concerns him." Elizabeth reached into her purse and pulled out a card with the Second-hand Blessings logo on it.

"Sure." He took the card and pressed it into his shirt pocket. "I'll be closing up in about half an hour. I'll be happy to give you a call." He gave her SUV a closer look. "And, for the record, if you're ever looking to trade this in for a newer model..."

"I'll know just where to come." Elizabeth flashed what she hoped looked like a convincing smile.

"In the meantime, if you want to talk to someone about that truck, just go around to the garage. It's in the back. Henri was the last person to see Jackson before he left, so you'll get your questions answered there. If you have any lingering questions, I mean."

"Henry?" Elizabeth cocked her head. "Who's he?"

"He's a she. Henrietta Sessions, my best mechanic. She's working on an older model BMW that just came in though, so don't get irritated if she doesn't take much time for you. I told her to rush it through for a new customer, and when she gets in the zone she doesn't like to be disturbed."

He rushed off, and Elizabeth faced her sister. "Well, what do you think? Should we go visit the mechanic to hear what she has to say?"

"Sure."

They rounded the building to the garage in the back. The whirring of machinery greeted them, along with the sight of an older model BMW up in the air on a lift.

Elizabeth wasn't sure what she was expecting Henri Sessions to look like, but the adorable, dark-haired young woman looked more like a college student than a rough-and-tumble mechanic. Her wavy hair was pulled back into a ponytail. She had those enviable long, dark lashes—not the kind so many girls stick on, but the real deal. If not for the dark blue work shirt with the Chester's Autos logo on it, Elizabeth would have guessed her to be a student headed to English class, not a mechanic with grease-stained hands.

The woman was hard at work on the BMW. Elizabeth tried to signal her, to get her attention.

"Hello!" Mary called out and waved her arms.

Henri turned. She pulled earbuds out of her ears and set down the wrench she'd been holding. "Oh, hey. Sorry, I didn't see you."

"Oh, it's okay," Elizabeth explained. "We're just—"

Fine lines formed around Henri's eyes. "Sorry, but we don't allow customers in the shop. Chester would kill me if he knew you were back here."

"Chester told us to come back," Mary said. "You're Henri?"

"I am." She swiped a loose strand of hair off her forehead with her fingertips. "How can I help you?"

"We're wondering if you remember a customer by the name of Jackson."

A smile lit Henri's face. "Red Ford F-150, 37,000 miles, V6, rear-wheel drive, automatic electronic eco boost, mud flaps, and American flag bumper sticker?"

"That's the one." Elizabeth laughed. "Guess you remember him, then."

Henri rested against the tire of the BMW. "I guess it's fair to say I remember the car more than the owner. That's often the case. But I did talk to him on Saturday when he dropped the truck off. He took off on foot and then came back because he'd left a picture in the glove compartment."

"And you say he left on foot?" Elizabeth asked.

Henri shrugged. "Well, I only saw him walk to the edge of the parking lot. Could be someone was meeting him or picking him up, or something like that."

"Did you find any clues about Jackson from his truck?" Mary asked.

"Clues?" Creases formed between Henri's carefully groomed brows. "Are you two detectives or something?"'

Elizabeth laughed. "No, nothing like that. We're actually sisters from Bird-in-Hand. We run a secondhand shop. We're trying to locate Jackson. He's a customer."

"Ah. Well, I can tell you that he took excellent care of his truck. Other than an oil change and tire rotation, I didn't have to do a thing to it. And it was clean as a whistle. Usually when vehicles come in here we pay a pretty penny to have them detailed, but in his case I didn't have to do a thing but vacuum it to get a little bit of dog hair off the front seat."

"So you met Rocky, then?"

"Yeah." A smile tipped up the edges of her lips. "Cute dog."

"What time would you say Jackson was here?"

"I know it was in the morning because it was before my lunch break. I'd already wrapped up the truck and was working on an SUV by the time I took a break to eat. I do remember that. Why?"

"Like I said, we're trying to track him down. For one thing, we've been worried about Rocky. He turned up at our shop on Saturday afternoon, and we're quite a distance away from here."

"Well, that's strange." Henri paused and gazed at the BMW. "I hate to cut this short, ladies, but I really need to get to work on this one before we close up shop. Was there anything else you needed?"

"No, not a thing." Elizabeth gave her a polite nod and then led the way out of the garage and back to the parking lot.

"Okay, so now what?" Mary asked.

"Now we wait on Chester to pay Jackson a visit, I guess."

"I guess." Mary's nose wrinkled. "And I guess we've learned a few things, anyway, so it wasn't a wasted trip. Rocky was with Jackson when he came in to sell the truck on Saturday morning."

"Right. But by Saturday afternoon the dog was at our shop, miles away. The question is, where did Jackson go after he left the car lot? Did he go home? If so, who drove him there?"

"Maybe he took an Uber or a cab," Mary suggested.

"I guess." Elizabeth shrugged. "I still can't wrap my head around the fact that the dog ended up at our store instead of with his owner if they were together at Chester's place earlier in the day."

She couldn't stop the questions from rolling around in her imagination. Something just didn't add up here.

Mary slid back behind the wheel of the SUV and settled into the seat. She buckled her seat belt and turned on the car, then faced Elizabeth. "At least we know Jackson's first name. Though, for the life of me, I don't know why we didn't think to ask his last name. What's wrong with us?"

"I think I was distracted by that salesman." Elizabeth buckled herself into the passenger seat and put her purse on the floorboard. "And by the time he told us he couldn't share Jackson's contact information, I didn't want to push things."

"Agreed." Mary pulled the visor down and checked her appearance. Ugh. Her face needed a little freshening. She reached into her purse and pulled out a tube of lipstick and smeared it on, then smacked her lips. There. That would do. She pressed the lipstick back into her purse, still focused on the matter at hand.

"I hate to sound cliché," Elizabeth said. "But at first I was sure Chester O'Conner was the poster boy for used-car salesmen."

"What do you mean?" Mary flipped the visor back up and then checked the rearview mirror.

"Oh, you know…the penetrating gaze. The fake smile. The lingo. He's got it all down. And I don't mind saying, he initially came across as totally disingenuous. Maybe it had something to do with that seersucker suit."

"Goodness. Tell me how you really feel, Lizzie." Mary chuckled as she reached for the gearshift. "You're not usually this outspoken about people."

"I know. He just gave me a weird vibe."

"Do you find everyone suspicious?"

Elizabeth nodded. "Only when there's a riddle to be solved."

"I suppose I see your point. His words were a little…"

"Fake?"

"Yeah. He was after one thing…the sale of that truck. Too bad for him we were here for something totally different." Mary shifted into reverse gear then glanced in her rearview mirror again and noticed a customer walking behind her car. She waited a moment and then eased the SUV backward.

"Still, we found the vehicle, and that's a good thing."

"And maybe he'll give us the information we're after. If he finds Jackson at home, he'll let us know."

"I don't know." Elizabeth shrugged. "I'm not saying I don't trust Chester. I don't even know the man. I would just feel better if I could see Jackson myself." She paused and then her voice grew more animated. "What would you think about following him?"

"Following Chester to Jackson's place, you mean?" Mary could barely contain her enthusiasm as she responded, "I thought you'd never ask."

CHAPTER SEVEN

Elizabeth held on to the arm of the passenger door as Mary changed from one lane to the other. Her heart raced nearly as fast as the speedometer. "Slow down a little," she said. "I'd like to make it there alive."

Mary tapped on the steering wheel in rhythm to the music on the radio. "Hey, I'm doing my best to keep up with Chester What's-his-name. Don't want to lose him, or we'll never find Jackson's house. I'm trying to keep my distance, but I don't want to lose sight of him."

"At this rate we'll probably run into him."

Mary slowed down a little. "There. Happy?"

"Mm-hmm. Do you think I should call Martha and let her know what we're doing?"

"The shop's already closed by now, remember?"

"Yes, but she'll be worried. We should at least call her to say we'll be late for supper."

"Sure." Mary lowered the volume on the radio.

Elizabeth reached for her phone and made the call. When she explained what they were up to, Martha released a loud sigh.

"I still can't believe you two are off having an adventure like that without me while I'm stuck here looking at cake pictures. Please be safe."

"We will." Elizabeth grimaced as Mary picked up speed again. "At least, I will. I can't speak for Mary. She's got the pedal to the metal like she's a NASCAR driver."

"Hey now!" Mary called out. "Don't exaggerate."

"Just keep me posted, okay?" Martha sounded more concerned than ever. "I'd like you both returned safely, please."

"We'll do our best."

Elizabeth ended the call and settled back against the seat. Hopefully they would arrive at Jackson's house soon, and in one piece, no less.

Mary continued to hum along with the radio, which she'd turned back up. A silence grew between the sisters as she continued to trail Chester O'Conner's vehicle. Elizabeth never minded the silences. In fact, she rather enjoyed them.

After a moment, Mary glanced her way. "Are you ever going to talk about it?"

"Hmm?" Elizabeth shook off her ponderings. "Talk about what?"

"You know what. The whole wedding thing. I can't help but think you're shying away from Anna's wedding plans because of your feelings about weddings in general. Don't think I haven't noticed that you've been keeping to yourself more than usual over the past few days. I think it's because we're all so excited about the wedding."

"Nothing could be further from the truth. Weddings are wonderful events, meant to be enjoyed." Elizabeth was surprised by the flood of emotions that swept over her as she spoke the words. "Sure, marriage wasn't in God's plans for me. I think we all know that. But that doesn't mean I would begrudge any other bride celebrating her big day. I hope I don't come across as that selfish."

"Of course not." Mary looked mortified at this suggestion. "I just want to make sure you're okay."

"I'm fine." She paused. "And please don't worry. I've reconciled myself to my situation, Mary. I really have. There are worse things in life than being single."

"It ain't over till it's over." Mary offered a playful wink. "If anyone deserves a happily ever after, it's you, Lizzie."

"I made my choice years ago. I just wasn't quite ready to marry Brenden and move off to Iowa, and he didn't want to wait for me. I can't really blame him. He had a wonderful job opportunity, and soon he found a lovely girl who was ready to marry. I confess, seeing Anna marry at her age, seeing what could have been, does cause me to flinch. A little. But I'm not looking back. Besides, Brenden is happily married, and I'm happy too." She shrugged and tried to push any negative emotions away. "Don't feel sorry for me, Mary. I'm at peace."

"Mm-hmm."

Just as Mary pulled the car off the highway onto a smaller, residential road, a call came through on Elizabeth's phone.

"Oh good, it's Susanna Wittmer." She took the call at once with a perky "Hello?"

"Elizabeth, this is Susanna. How are you?"

"I'm fine. I—"

"I know you are interested in the washbasin, but I really meant what I said that day at the auction…it is definitely not for sale."

"Oh, no…I—"

"It is a family heirloom and very valuable. If we ever decide to sell it, I will let you know, but even then, we would probably go through a dealer, since it is worth quite a bit of money. It is a Foley Wileman. A very rare piece. I am sure you understand."

"Oh, I do. Better than you know. I really just wanted to ask you—"

"I am sorry, Elizabeth, I must go. I am sorry to get your hopes up about the washbasin."

And at that, the call ended.

Elizabeth did her best not to groan aloud as she pressed her cell phone back into her purse. "Oh brother."

"What did she say?" Mary asked.

"She still thinks I want to buy the washbasin from her. And she was firm about it, didn't even give me a chance to get a word in edgewise. She wanted to let me know it's not available. And it's definitely a Foley Wileman."

"Let's just go out there and visit with her in person," Mary suggested. "Tomorrow, when things slow down?"

"Sure. Tomorrow." Elizabeth thought through their plan, hesitating. "Only, we left Martha alone in the store this afternoon, so maybe it's not such a good idea to leave her again tomorrow."

"I'll watch the store. You can go visit Susanna on your own."

"Okay."

Mary followed at a distance behind Chester's car as he pulled into a neighborhood labeled Clearview.

"Looks like we're getting close." Elizabeth turned her attention out of the window to the houses on her right. "This is one of the older neighborhoods in Lancaster, looks like."

"I'm guessing these houses were built in the '40s or '50s." Mary slowed the car to keep her distance behind Chester.

He pulled his vehicle up to a small wood-framed house in a faded tan color.

Mary pulled to the curb several houses away, but Elizabeth had enough of a view to tell that Jackson's house was in rundown condition, at best.

Chipped paint, a cracked window at the front of the house, yard overgrown. Interesting. Not what she was expecting, based on the condition of his vehicle, but who was she to judge?

"Chester's getting out of his car, Mary. Look." She pointed.

"Yes, I see him. I hope he doesn't get bitten by a snake. That grass is high."

They watched in silence as he made his way to the front door. He appeared to be knocking, but no one responded. After a few minutes, Chester gave up and walked back to his car. A couple of minutes later, Elizabeth's phone rang. She gasped when she looked down and saw Chester's number.

"Go ahead and answer it," Mary said. "He has no idea we're right behind him."

Elizabeth tried to steady her voice as she took the call. "H-hello?"

"Hi there. This is Chester from Chester's Autos."

"Yes, Chester. How are you?"

"Fine. Just wanted you to know that I drove out to Jackson's place, and he's not home. I'm going to leave a note on the door, but the house doesn't look like anyone's been in it for a while."

"Strange."

"Very. I'm worried about him. And I don't see any sign of Rocky, so I'm worried about him too. If I hear anything I'll let you know. I just wanted to update you, in the meantime."

"We appreciate you checking on him for us, Chester. Thanks for the update." She pushed the button to end the call and then watched as Chester went back up to the door and stuck some sort of paper by the knob. As he pulled away from the front of the house a few minutes later, Elizabeth breathed a sigh of relief.

"Well, that was awkward," she said.

"Yeah. But I'm still not convinced Jackson isn't home." Mary pulled the SUV up to the front of Jackson's house. "Just because a yard is overgrown and a person doesn't answer the door doesn't mean he's not really there. Could be he doesn't want to talk to anyone."

"How will we know?"

"I say we go up to the door ourselves and try knocking."

Nerves took hold of Elizabeth, and her stomach fluttered. "I don't know, Mary."

"Come on. What's the worst that could happen?"

Elizabeth could think of quite a few things, actually, but didn't voice them aloud. Instead, she followed on her sister's heels as Mary marched up the front walk, past the overgrown yard, over a broken potted plant, and beyond the weeds coming up through the cracks in the concrete.

Elizabeth kept her distance, but admired her sister's tenacity.

"Man, this place could use some TLC."

"No kidding." Elizabeth stepped over a garden hose, which had been looped over the walkway.

Mary knocked—a firm "we're here to do business" knock—but no one answered. A couple of minutes later she tried again, but they were still left hanging.

"Either he really, really doesn't want to be interrupted or he's not here."

"Or something's wrong with him," Elizabeth countered. "He didn't look very good when I saw him on Saturday, Mary. What if he's in there, sick. Or...dead?"

"Don't let your imagination run away with you, Elizabeth."

"It's hard not to. Maybe we could leave a note on the door," Elizabeth suggested.

Mary pointed to the card Chester had left. "We don't want to overwhelm him. If he ever does show up at home he'll wonder why the troops have all been sent to find him."

"Maybe."

They turned back toward the car and had nearly made it when an elderly man next door waved at them.

"He's been gone for days, ladies," the man hollered.

"Jackson? He's moved out?" Elizabeth took a few steps toward the man. He had one of those soft white mustaches, so thin that you could barely call it a mustache at all. It matched the beard, also thinning and pale.

"Fred Zucker." The man came toward them and extended a shaky hand. His gray-blue eyes twinkled, as if he was up to some sort of mischief.

Elizabeth shook his hand. "I'm Elizabeth Classen, and this is my sister Mary."

"You're looking for Jackson?" The fellow's brows elevated.

"Yes. We have a few questions for him. Any idea when he'll be back?"

The man's expression shifted to one of concern. "I was hoping you were going to tell me that. I've been worried sick about him. He's been gone three days. It's very strange." Mr. Zucker coughed—one of those deep, rattly "I've had too many cigarettes" coughs. "Nothing's adding up. I picked him up after he sold the truck."

"You did?"

"Well, sure. He needed a way home from the car lot. I met him at a gas station not too far from there. Brought him home. Thought he was here to stay, but he took off on foot around noon, claiming he needed something from the grocery store. I haven't seen him since. It's just not like him to disappear like that. We've been neighbors for years, and I know him as well as I know myself. He wouldn't just leave and not come back."

His words certainly didn't ease Elizabeth's concerns.

Mr. Zucker wagged his finger in the air. "And I don't mind saying, I'm a little leery of that fella who just stopped by, that Chester fella. The one who bought Jackson's truck from him."

"Why?" Mary asked.

"Because he pestered Jackson for weeks to sell him that truck. I tried to talk him out of it. I knew Jackson needed the money, but that truck was his pride and joy, one of the few things he had left after the divorce. It meant a lot to him. Giving it up was kind of like admitting defeat. You know?"

"That's sad," Elizabeth said.

"Yep. All I know is, everything changed on the day he sold that truck." Mr. Zucker shifted his gaze to Jackson's house. "I've tried his cell phone, his house phone...nothing. And trust me, I've been keeping a close eye on his place. Until today, I haven't seen a soul. Then, suddenly, you gals show up. And Chester too. He was just here."

"But no sign of Jackson," Mary said.

"Right. No idea why he's suddenly disappeared or where he's gone."

"Or why Rocky was on the loose Saturday afternoon," Elizabeth added.

"Rocky?" Mr. Zucker grew more animated. "You know Rocky?"

"Yes," Mary said. "He showed up at our shop in Bird-in-Hand on Saturday afternoon with no collar. He came tearing into the place like he owned it, then shot back out the door and disappeared down the highway."

Mr. Zucker's jaw dropped. "Well, I'll be. That explains *that*. You'll be happy to know he made it back home. But it helps to know where he wandered off to." He chuckled. "I don't mind telling you, I was worried sick about him. Really gave me a scare, him being gone all those hours."

"Made it back home?" Elizabeth shifted her gaze back to Jackson's house. "He's...he's here?"

Mr. Zucker pointed to his own front door. Through the glass, Elizabeth caught a glimpse of the boxer, leaping up and down. "Yep, Rocky's home." He rested his hands on his hips. "Right where he belongs."

CHAPTER EIGHT

Elizabeth stared at the dog, dumbfounded. What was Rocky doing here, at Mr. Zucker's place? The hyper pup continued to jump up and down, yipping and yapping from the other side of the glass, and she wondered how she hadn't noticed him before.

"Want to come in and say hello to my boy?" Mr. Zucker asked. "He's not gonna rest until I open that door. And if you know Rocky, you know how feisty he can be."

"Sure do." Elizabeth glanced over at Mary, who nodded, wide-eyed. No doubt she was equally confused.

They followed Mr. Zucker to the front door. Mary mouthed the words "What in the world?" but Elizabeth just shrugged. She had no idea. None of this made sense. Perhaps Mr. Zucker could shed some light on things for them once they got inside.

Inside.

Should they really go inside a stranger's home? How did they know this man was trustworthy? Elizabeth could almost picture the expression on John's face once he found out. Still, there was no turning back now, not if they wanted to get the information about the dog.

Mr. Zucker opened the door, and the dog bounded out onto the front walkway. Rocky seemed to recognize the ladies right away. With the same boisterous energy as ever, he jumped up and put his front two paws on Elizabeth's chest, then started licking her face. *Ick.* She did her best to push him away, but the pooch persisted in making his presence known.

"Whoa, Rocky. Down, boy." Mr. Zucker squinted past his reading glasses and then pulled the dog off of her. "Sorry, ladies. He's still on a learning curve, but we're working on his manners. He has a long way to go yet."

So strange. Why did the man talk about Rocky as if he owned him?

"Oh, it's okay," Elizabeth said, and she nudged the dog down. "I understand. We have dogs too."

"Bet they're not this crazy." Mr. Zucker laughed.

"No," Mary agreed, "they're not."

Mr. Zucker gestured for them to enter his house. Elizabeth was a little nervous about stepping inside. She looked back at Mary, whose movements could best be described as tentative. What did they know about this man, anyway? He could be a criminal for all they knew.

Calm yourself, Elizabeth.

She did her best not to hyperfocus on the man as she and Mary followed him into the front hallway. His bald head, smooth as a billiard ball, was splattered with tiny age spots. And his oversized ears seemed ill-placed on a man with no hair to cover them up. She blinked and looked away, not wanting to stare.

Only then did she notice the chaos that was his living room. It reminded her of a *Hoarders* episode, only tidier, if such a thing were possible. Rows of shelves lined the walls, much like in Secondhand Blessings. Each shelf was loaded with stuff. Lots and lots of stuff—everything from miniature cars and tiny planes to a variety of military items. It appeared to be semiorganized, albeit dusty. The table was covered in clutter as well, and the floor was stacked with boxes and bins, most labeled as collectibles of some sort or another. He'd covered every square inch of wall space with signs—everything from old gas station signs to road signs. Very…eclectic.

"I know, I know…" He gestured to the clutter and groaned. "It started innocently, ladies. I collected car memorabilia from the fifties and sixties. Then, after a while, I guess my hobby just sort of took over. I developed an interest in planes. And, of course, I love all things military. I was in the Marines. Jackson and I have that in common."

"Semper Fi." Elizabeth gave him a little salute, and he smiled. She glanced at the end table and noticed a couple of pairs of reading glasses.

Mr. Zucker dove into a conversation about his years in the Gulf War. Elizabeth hated to stop him, but she wondered how long this story would take. She watched as he walked to the sofa and pushed several newspapers aside. If he was clearing a spot for her to sit, she would have to beg off. No way was she going to sit on that sofa. Underneath the papers the cushions were covered in dog hair. Just about the time he got that section of the sofa cleared, Rocky jumped up onto it, turned in a couple of circles, and planted himself in the clean spot, as comfortably as if he'd done it a thousand times before.

None of this made sense.

"Get off of there, Rocky," Mr. Zucker scolded. "How many times do I have to tell you we don't get on the sofa unless we're given permission?"

Judging from the dog hair, Rocky was given permission...a lot.

Elizabeth waved her hand. "That's okay, Mr. Zucker."

"Fred."

"Fred." She smiled. "We've been sitting in the car all this way. I need to stretch my legs."

Mary's eyes widened as she looked at the sofa. "Same here. I'd just as soon stand too."

"Suit yourself." He sat in the recliner and tilted it back. Underneath the glow of the overhead lamp, his bald head glistened. He pressed his glasses up to the bridge of his nose and rested his hands behind his head. "I didn't mean to talk your ears off, ladies. I don't get a lot of company around here. This house sits empty most of the time, 'cept when Jackson comes around. Guess I was in need of some company."

"It's no problem," Elizabeth said.

His easy smile tilted downward into a frown. "Now, you said you had some questions about Jackson?"

"We do," Elizabeth said. "We're looking for him because he brought an item into our resale shop last week, and we have some questions about it."

"I'm not surprised he came to your shop. He's been selling off a bunch of his belongings since he lost his job last spring." Fred gestured around the living room. "Shoot, a bunch of the stuff in my house was his to begin with—the bed in my guest room, that table over there..." He gestured to a scarred oak table with four chairs. "And my favorite recliner." He patted the arm of his chair. "All his. Until a few months ago, when things started getting bad for him."

"Oh, wow." Elizabeth shook her head. "I'm sorry to hear that."

"Me too. I've felt pretty sorry for the guy. He's been down on his luck for a while now and things don't seem to be getting better, especially this past week or so."

"What happened this past week?" Elizabeth asked.

"I don't know details, but I think he's about to lose his house to the bank. That's why he sold the truck, to catch up on mortgage payments. But I don't know if he managed to do that or not, since he disappeared on me."

"That's awful," Mary said.

"Yep. I did what I could to help out. Every time Jackson needed money to pay the utilities I'd buy something else off of him." Fred pointed to Rocky snoozing on the couch. "He's my best purchase yet."

Elizabeth's breath caught in her throat. "You bought Rocky from him?"

"Sure did. He needed the money, and—to be honest—I needed a friend. I'm all alone in this big house with no one to talk to but the TV. Rocky makes a great companion. He's a good guard dog too."

Elizabeth looked at Mary and saw the same sad look on her face she knew was on her own. Did anyone willingly give up a beloved pet unless they were absolutely at the end of their rope?

"Could I offer you ladies a glass of water?" Fred's voice snapped her to attention.

"Oh, no, thank you." Elizabeth glanced at the clock on the wall. 5:50. Ugh. "We have to get back home, actually. It's a bit of a drive to our farm."

"Where did you say you live?"

"Bird-in-Hand," Elizabeth responded. "Off Ronks Road."

"Quite a distance."

"Yes."

Mary shuffled her purse from one shoulder to the other, probably a quiet signal that she was ready to go. Elizabeth didn't blame her. This whole thing was rather uncomfortable.

"Still can't get over the fact that Rocky made it all the way there and back on his own." Fred scratched the pooch behind the ear. "He's got an amazing homing device built-in, I guess. Me? I can't find my reading glasses or the morning paper. Might've been better off if I'd been born a dog." He got tickled at his own joke and started laughing.

"I guess that's one way to look at it." Mary shifted her position, clearly ready to bolt.

Mr. Zucker didn't seem to notice. Judging by the sparkle in his eyes he was enjoying the conversation. "I watched a movie about a dog that found his way home, even though he was thousands of miles away. Not saying I believe that's really possible, but it made for an exciting movie."

"Well, thank you for visiting with us, Fred," Mary said, her gaze shifting to the front door. "We're grateful for any information you might have about Jackson. Can I give you my card so you can call us if he turns up or if you hear from him?"

"Of course. I sure hope he does turn up, and I'll let you know if I see him, I promise."

"We hope he does too," Elizabeth said.

Mary gave him a business card, and he adjusted his glasses to read it. "Secondhand Blessings, eh? I think I've driven past that place. It's in a barn, right?"

"Right," Elizabeth said. "If you've been to Bird-in-Hand, you've probably driven by it."

"I'll have to come visit sometime." Fred laughed and gestured around the room. "Not that I need to be adding to this mess, but you never know. I might find a few treasures."

"Yes. And if you ever decide to purge, we take items on consignment." Mary's voice was all business now. "Might be a good way to pare down your stash and make a little cash."

"Pare down your stash and make a little cash." He slapped his knee and chuckled. "Now that's a slogan. I say you put that on a billboard to advertise the place."

"Sounds like something Mama would've come up with," Mary said.

"Sure does." Elizabeth looked down at the oak table and noticed a couple more pairs of reading glasses. Spares for when he misplaced them, she supposed.

As he rose from his recliner, Fred let out a groan and put his hand on his back. "It ain't easy gettin' old, ladies. I recommend you avoid it if you can." Elizabeth didn't have a chance to respond—which was just as well—because he kept his end of the conversation in full swing as he walked them to the door.

Rocky jumped up and nuzzled against Elizabeth, whimpering nonstop. She reached down to pat him on the head, but had to wonder why the pooch was so discontent.

"Now stop that, boy." Fred tugged on his collar. "These ladies don't need your affection."

Collar.

For the first time, Elizabeth realized the dog was wearing a collar today, but it was a different one from the sturdy green one he'd been wearing that first day. This one was blue and much narrower.

The dog continued to whine, and Fred kept scolding him. "Sorry he's being such a nuisance. Rocky's usually pretty calm, but these past few days he's been really worked up."

Likely missing his former owner, but Elizabeth wouldn't say that aloud. She didn't want to hurt Fred's feelings. He clearly loved the dog.

"Thanks again for your help." Mary opened the door and stepped outside.

Elizabeth said her goodbyes and then joined Mary on the front walkway. In just the few minutes they'd been in the house, the sun had begun dipping low in the sky to their left.

Fred flipped on his porch light and waved. "You ladies be safe driving back. I'll call if I hear anything." He closed the door behind him.

"Well, that was different." Elizabeth shook her head. "This day just gets stranger and stranger."

"No kidding." Mary led the way to the car, carrying on about all of the items in Fred Zucker's house. "I hope he decides to sell off some of that stuff. My mind was reeling. It was all I could do not to go through everything, piece by piece."

"His house did feel a bit like a store," Elizabeth agreed. "He probably would have loved it if we'd stayed and looked over his treasures, but I'm ready to get back home. It's been a long day."

"Agreed. And we're really no closer to tracking down Jackson to ask him about that pitcher."

"Right. I'm disappointed about that." As they walked to the car Elizabeth's thoughts kept jumping around. She thought about what Fred had said about Jackson disappearing. Where was he? Was he okay?

She opened the passenger side door and climbed inside, her thoughts still tumbling. "I just don't know, Mary," she said as her sister took her place behind the wheel. "Fred Zucker seems safe enough. But I'm still not totally convinced."

"I know. I can't understand how a person could give up their dog. I know I never could, no matter what circumstances I was in."

"I know, and that's what worries me. Was Jackson that desperate? Is Fred Zucker telling the truth? Jackson is missing. He sold his truck. The house sits empty. The neighbor has the dog. And we have the expensive porcelain pitcher that may or may not have been his to begin with. The whole thing is just so…"

"Mysterious?" Mary set her purse down on the console between them.

"Yes." Elizabeth fastened her seatbelt, deep in thought. "Maybe it's not our story to figure out though. You know? I'm already feeling like we've overstepped by coming to Jackson's house in the first place. In fact, I'm starting to feel like a real snoop."

Mary adjusted the rearview mirror and slid the key into the car's ignition. "Yes, and it's getting late. I've still got some wedding details to go over this evening. I should get back and put in a couple of hours on that. Not to mention the fact that Martha needs baking powder from the store. Remember?"

"Oh, that's right. I'm getting hungry, so I sure hope she kept supper warm." As the rumbling of the car's engine kicked in, Elizabeth leaned back against the seat, her gaze firmly fixed on Jackson's house and the overgrown yard. Off in the distance the setting sun cast its final golden rays. She squinted to take in the dented metal mailbox. Only when she gave it a closer look did she make out the faded letters spelling out Jackson's last name. As it came into view, she could scarcely believe her eyes.

Wittmer.

Jackson's last name was Wittmer.

CHAPTER NINE

The following morning Elizabeth woke up early and spent time praying and reading her Bible. She wanted to push all thoughts of Jackson out of her mind, at least while she spent time with the Lord, but her mind would not rest. Why had Jackson disappeared?

For sure, she needed to contact Susanna today to ask about the Wittmer connection. If Jackson was a part of the larger Wittmer family, then perhaps all of this made sense on some deeper level. Perhaps he was with them, even now. Perhaps they had decided that the Foley Wileman pitcher could be sold, and they'd just hang on to the basin.

On the other hand, Wittmer was a fairly common name in this area. In fact, there were Wittmers all over Lancaster County. There might not be any connection at all. If he was related to them, he would never have sold a family heirloom. Right?

Perhaps she should look Jackson up on social media. If he had an account, maybe there would be clues there. She would do so later, when things calmed down.

For now, though, she needed to stay focused on the shop. Mary and Martha had gone above and beyond over the past couple of work days, managing things without her. Today she would stay put and do whatever was needed in the store.

Sometime around ten thirty the ladies gathered in the stockroom to look over the items Mary had pulled aside for Anna's wedding. She had managed to find quite an assortment of decorative bits that all looked perfect for the bride-to-be's big day.

"Anna is going to be stopping by with Wayne at noon," Mary explained. "He's bringing a truck to haul this stuff to the barn. So I need to make sure you're both in agreement about what we'll be lending her."

"Wayne?" Elizabeth didn't recognize the name.

"You remember—the groom-to-be," Mary explained. "He came by on Saturday afternoon when you were at the auction."

"Oh, right, the doctor."

"Yes. He seems like a really great guy. Anyway, I need to make sure we're all onboard with loaning these items for the wedding. How do you feel about it?"

Elizabeth didn't really mind. In fact, once she saw the pieces all arranged in the stockroom, she could almost imagine how beautiful the reception was going to be. If farmhouse chic was the latest trend, then Anna would be the trendiest bride in town.

Before she could say so, the front door of the shop opened and a new round of shoppers entered—this time, a bus full of senior citizens from a nearby retirement center. They *oohed* and *aahed* over many of the items, and several of them made purchases.

Just after the crowd thinned, Elizabeth's cell phone rang. She didn't recognize the number but took the call anyway, hoping it wasn't a telemarketer. A male voice greeted her on the other end of the line, a vaguely familiar voice.

"Which of you two gals am I talking to?" Fred Zucker asked. "Can't rightly remember which of you gave me the business card."

"This is Elizabeth Classen, Mr. Zucker."

"Fred."

"This is Elizabeth, Fred."

"That's better. Now, are you the one who was wearing the bright pink shirt and jeans or the one in the blue blouse and slacks?"

"Blue blouse."

"Okay. Needed to know who I was talking to. I thought you ladies would like to know that someone stopped by Jackson's place today while I was out mowing my lawn."

"Oh?" This piqued Elizabeth's curiosity. "Who's that?"

"His ex-wife, Emily. She marched through that front door like she owned the place. Just thought you'd want to know."

"Well, I don't want to judge her. Maybe she does still own the place, at least half of it."

"Not sure about that. She hasn't been around in ages. Kind of surprised me to see her there. I watched her from my side yard. I don't think she noticed. She hauled out a few things— looked like some knickknacks and such. Seemed kind of strange, like she knew Jackson wasn't going to be there. She came and went pretty freely."

"Are they still in communication?"

"Not that I know of. Last time he talked to me about Emily, he said they hadn't spoken in months, except through their attorneys. That's another fella he owes money to, his attorney. But I guess that's a story for another day."

"Right. That's interesting." Though Elizabeth felt a bit like a gossip talking about all of this. Jackson and his ex-wife certainly didn't need her censure.

Fred rambled on, his words more amped up as he went. "After Emily left, I went over there for a little look-see. The front door was unlocked. Found that kind of strange, but I was scared to lock it, in case Jackson showed back up without a key or something like that. I just don't know what to do, now that he's been gone. Rocky and I are both a mess."

"Fred, if Jackson is really missing, don't you think you should call the police? File a missing-person report?"

He sighed. "I've been thinking about that very thing. Guess I'm the logical candidate to do so. I'm about the closest thing he's got to family, now that Emily is out of the picture. I keep trying his cell, but there's no answer. It just goes straight to voice mail."

She could hear Rocky barking in the background.

"Get out of that window, dog!" Fred called out. "You're tearing up my blinds!" His voice faded as he disappeared from the call for a moment. When he returned, he sounded out of breath. "Not sure I'm meant to be a dog owner, to be honest. I love him. I really do. But this canine is a lot of work." Fred paused. "Not that you can get rid of a family member, of course. He's like a baby, this crazy oaf. I'm just not used to having him underfoot yet."

"Speaking of family… Did you ever hear Jackson mention any family from Bird-in-Hand? Amish folks?"

"Amish?" Fred laughed. "He's about the furthest thing from Amish. Very into technology. The man loves his computers.

And that truck was his pride and joy. Can't picture him being raised Amish. He's more likely to tell you how to rewire a thermostat than to plow the ground."

"But he's a Wittmer, and we have some Amish neighbors who are Wittmers."

"I know a dozen Wittmers, and none of 'em are Amish. Neither is Jackson."

"So he never mentioned his family—even cousins or something like that."

"Nope. Just Emily…and the baby."

This took her by surprise. "They have a baby?"

"Had." Fred hesitated. "She was a toddler, actually. A little girl. She passed when she was only two years old. Something called RSV, I think?"

"That's awful."

"Yeah, I just remember it devastated Jackson. And Emily too. They were never the same after that."

"I can't even imagine. Well, thank you for sharing all of this, Fred. I'm grateful." Elizabeth paused and thought of one last thing she needed to address. "Oh, before we go, I have a couple of questions about the dog. I forgot to mention yesterday that we spoke to the man who bought the truck from Jackson."

"You talked to that Chester fella?"

"Yes. And with his mechanic too. They both saw Rocky with Jackson last Saturday morning. Do you mind if I ask when you bought him?"

"Well… See, it's like this. I bought the dog from Jackson awhile back, but didn't take possession of him until Saturday."

"What do you mean?"

"I just didn't have the heart. I paid Jackson for him and took him home a couple of weeks ago, but Rocky always ended up whining and carrying on until his real master got home. I could see where his heart was, so I told Jackson to keep him until he absolutely had to give him up, even though my house was too quiet for my liking without him. On Saturday Jackson called and asked if I could pick him and Rocky up at the gas station, about a block from the car shop. I picked them up around ten thirty and brought them back to his house. I think I said before, Jackson stuck around until about noon. Then he said he needed something from the store. He took off, and I guess I dozed off. Rocky must have got out from under the back fence not long after Jackson left. I figured the dog had gone looking for him."

"Makes sense, especially if he left on foot."

"Right. And the grocery store's only a couple of blocks away. It wouldn't be the first time Jackson walked down there. He likes too, well…" Fred paused. "Look, if we're being real, I might as well tell you. He drinks a little. When he's got money to buy a twelve-pack, I mean. And that day he had money because he'd just sold the truck. So I guess he felt like drowning his sorrows in a beer or two. Or ten."

"My goodness."

"Yeah." Fred sighed. "Once he gets started, it's hard to get him to stop. I've witnessed it firsthand."

Elizabeth couldn't even imagine it, but people did struggle with such things.

"Now, I'm not saying I blame him when he binges like that," Fred added. "He's been through a lot, after all. And if I'm being completely honest, I shared a few drinks with him on occasion. But no one can put away beer like Jackson can. He's a pro at it."

Elizabeth cringed. "So he was drinking on Saturday after he sold the truck?"

"I wasn't in the house with him, but I'm guessing so because he told me he'd run out of beer and needed to go to the store to get more." Fred sighed. "Anyway, he never came back from the store, and then the dog got out, as I said. Late Saturday night I found Rocky on Jackson's front porch, crying."

"That's heartbreaking."

"Tell me about it." Fred sounded more distressed than ever. "Anyway, I finally got him inside, but it took him forever to calm down. I think the poor thing wore himself out worrying over Jackson."

"Did you give any thought to calling the police?"

"Sure, but you can't really fault a guy for not coming home for a night or two. For all I know, he could be off staying with a new girlfriend or something. You know what I mean? That's really none of my business, so why interfere or ask questions?"

"Would he really head to a new girlfriend's house on foot?"

"I don't know. And to be honest, the girlfriend theory probably wouldn't hold water. He's still hung up on his wife. Ex-wife. Emily. He can't seem to shake his feelings for her, I guess. It happens like that sometimes, even after divorce."

"Please call the police. I'll feel much better knowing someone is looking for Jackson."

"Good idea. I will too." He paused. "Well, it was good to talk to you, Elizabeth in the blue blouse. You and that sister of yours feel free to come visit me anytime. Or better yet, I'll come visit you with a carful of collectibles from my house."

"Please do. We'll look forward to it."

After she ended the call, Elizabeth waited on another round of customers. Still, she couldn't stop thinking through what she'd just learned. Was Jackson still in love with his ex-wife? Why had Emily shown up at his house? And why had Rocky come all that way to Bird-in-Hand, only to return home again?

When she found herself alone at the register, Elizabeth reached for her laptop. She signed on to her Facebook account and did a quick search for a Jackson Wittmer. It took a bit of scrolling before she located the correct one. She had to weed her way through all of the other J. Wittmers in the Lancaster area, which was quite a task. It turned out there were several, as if she needed any confirmation that the Wittmer name was popular in this area. But she located his page and looked through some of his photos, just to make sure. It was him. The man in the pictures with a woman and little girl looked like he was on top of the world. Jackson Wittmer had seen better days.

Elizabeth scrolled down his page. She wasn't able to see all of his posts, since they weren't friends, but she could see enough to know she had the right man. She had to smile when she saw a picture of him standing in front of the red truck with Rocky beside him. He definitely loved that dog. And he must have been mighty proud of that truck too. Otherwise, why pose in front of it?

She felt sorry for the guy. Really sorry. He'd lost both—the dog and the truck. On top of his wife and daughter. What was his wife's name again? Emily? Out of curiosity, she pulled up his friends list. Maybe she could link him back to Susanna Wittmer this way.

No, wait. Susanna and her brothers weren't active on social media. They were Old Order Amish, not *Englischers*.

Still, she scrolled through Jackson's friends list and stopped when she came across the name Emily Wittmer. It seemed a bit strange that a divorced couple would remain friends on social media, but there she was—a lovely woman with shoulder-length blond hair and a bright smile, the same woman she'd seen in Jackson's photos. Her headshot revealed a real beauty, complete with perfect makeup and trendy clothes. If Elizabeth hadn't known they'd been married, she would never have guessed them to be a couple. They seemed worlds apart.

She clicked to Elizabeth's profile and saw that she worked for a local real estate firm. Interesting, especially in light of the fact that Jackson was about to lose his house.

Elizabeth didn't feel comfortable sending Emily a friend request, but she did wonder if they had any mutual friends. A quick search revealed that they did not. Elizabeth went to Emily's photo albums and there, tucked away between wedding photos and a couple of pictures of Jackson and Rocky, were photos of the same beautiful little girl with blond curls and dimples. The adorable toddler had the brightest blue eyes, and her skin was as lovely as porcelain.

The words *Rest in Peace, Sophia* were stamped across the top of the photo. It was all Elizabeth could do not to cry as she read them.

No wonder Jackson was a broken man. No wonder he drowned his sorrows in alcohol. To lose someone this innocent, this precious, would be completely devastating.

Elizabeth backed out of Emily's page and clicked to Jackson's friends list. One last skim revealed Fred Zucker's name. She couldn't help but smile when she saw it. What a sweet old guy he'd turned out to be.

She followed the link to his account and browsed his most recent public posts.

One post made yesterday included a picture of Rocky. Underneath it was the caption, "My new BFF."

CHAPTER TEN

Martha looked up from her laptop as Mary entered the stockroom. She'd stared at so many wedding cake pictures her vision was blurry. She managed a quiet, "Hey there," then rubbed her eyes and shut the laptop.

"You haven't figured that cake out yet?" Mary asked. "Please don't tell me Anna is still sending you photos."

"Yeah. It's crazy. And I'm sorry it's taking so much time away from the shop. I promise, I won't let it consume me."

Mary gave her a sympathetic look followed by the wave of a hand. "You're apologizing to me, after all the time I've spent searching for decor for Anna? I don't mind. Seriously. You've done more than your fair share lately."

"You know me. I'm a doer. I'm not happy unless I'm going, going, going. Just how I'm wired, I guess."

Mary laughed. "Actually, I was just about to ask if you were ready to take a lunch break. And I love that we're both able to help Anna. I'm sure she appreciates it. And look on the bright side—the wedding will be over in a few days. Things will get back to normal around here. Our version of it, anyway."

"Thanks. I'm sure Elizabeth will be glad when it's behind us. Sometimes I think she's a little sensitive where weddings are concerned." Truth be told, Martha had secretly wondered if this whole thing was too much for Elizabeth to take. Mary too, for that matter.

Mary shrugged. "I asked her about that when we were driving to Lancaster. She seems to have a pretty good attitude about it all, actually. I wouldn't worry too much about her. She's come a long way over the years. I'm proud of her."

"Me too. And you?" Martha gave Mary a closer look. "You're doing okay?"

"You know me, I always bounce back. Life doesn't get me down for long. And I can certainly celebrate with a friend who's getting married, even if my own marriage caused pain."

The ladies took a seat at the table in the stockroom and ate together while Elizabeth covered the register. They spent most of their time going over details for the upcoming wedding. When they wrapped up, Martha decided this would be the perfect time to ask Mary about last night's outing to Lancaster.

"So you and Elizabeth had quite the adventure last night, she tells me."

"Yes." Mary dabbed at her lips with a napkin. "You would have loved Fred Zucker's house, Martha. His shelves were even more loaded than ours at the shop. It was crazy. But kind of cool. He has a lot of great items."

"Some people are like that. Pack rats."

"He was more of a collector. I'm sure some of it is worth a pretty penny. He's got a lot of money invested in that stuff."

"Wish I'd seen it for myself." Martha wrapped up what was left of her sandwich and set it aside. She took a drink from her water bottle and settled back in her chair.

"It was something to see. That's for sure. I have to wonder if he's lonely. Maybe he's trying to replace people with stuff. You know?"

Elizabeth appeared in the doorway holding her open laptop. She looked frenzied.

Martha sat up straight in her chair. "Everything okay?"

"Yes." Elizabeth brushed into the room and put the laptop on the table. "Just wanted to share something I discovered online."

"What's that?" Martha asked.

Elizabeth turned her laptop in their direction and pointed at the screen. Martha could make out the blue and white colors of someone's Facebook account.

"What are we looking at?" she asked.

Elizabeth pointed to the screen. "I've been doing a little snooping, and I found Fred Zucker's Facebook page."

"Anything of interest?" Martha asked. "I heard about his collectibles. Mary was just telling me."

"Well, I'm able to see the groups he's joined. Most are for collectors of the things we saw in his house—cars, planes, and so on." Elizabeth shrugged. "The saddest part about his Facebook page is that he has absolutely no family listed—no wife, no children, no grandchildren. Don't you find that strange?"

Martha stared at her older sister. Did she really not hear the irony in what she just said? She raised her eyebrows. "Well, um…it happens, Lizzie. Some people never marry." She regretted the words as soon as she said them when she saw the look on Elizabeth's face.

Elizabeth did her best not to read too much into her sister's words. Martha wasn't trying to be inconsiderate. She was just making a point.

"Clearly, some people never marry." Elizabeth pointed to herself. "Exhibit A."

"I'm sorry, Lizzie," Martha said. "I didn't mean—"

"No, don't worry. My point is that more often than not it's women who remain single. So when you do find an older single man, you have to assume he's a bit of an anomaly."

"I've known a few single men in that age group," Mary said. "But most of 'em get snatched up by older single ladies lickety-split."

Elizabeth nodded. "Right. I'm just saying that all of those collections make sense when you realize there are no people to fill the void in his life."

"We were just talking about that, actually," Martha said. "But you've confirmed it."

"And it also explains why he's taken such an interest in Jackson," Mary chimed in. "My take is that he's a very lonely old man."

"Just so sad." Elizabeth's gaze shifted to the floor and then back up again. "You know, sometimes I feel a little sorry for myself because I never married and don't have children. But I look around me and see so many people in my world—my sisters, friends, church folks. And of course all of my nieces and nephews." Her heart warmed at the mention of the kids. "God has filled in the gaps with people I love and people who love me."

"Of course He has." Mary got up and rested her hand on Elizabeth's arm. "And aren't we blessed to have so many young ones coming up behind us? Those kiddos are going to do great things."

"They are," Elizabeth agreed. "They're far more important than anything we'll ever collect in this store."

"Well, of course they are," Mary agreed.

"And though some might think I'm into things"—she gestured to the items on the stockroom shelves—"nothing could be further from the truth. I'm pretty plain Jane. I'll take people any day over things."

"Amen to that," Mary said. "But test me on that. Offer me diamonds and pearls, and see if I turn them down."

This got a laugh out of all the sisters.

Mary and Martha took over the register, and Elizabeth decided to take her lunch break. She toyed with the notion of going to see Susanna but didn't think she would have enough time. Instead, she rushed through her meal then returned to the store, where she helped her sisters stock the shelves with more incoming items. Her mind kept drifting back to the washbasin. Oh, if only she could have another peek. Was the design the same...really?

By the time the last customer pulled out of the parking lot at two o'clock, Elizabeth was completely exhausted. She couldn't seem to stop yawning.

"You okay over there?" Mary gave her an inquisitive look.

"Mm-hmm. Not sure why I'm so tired."

"Well, thank goodness it's Tuesday, right?" Mary countered. "You can head back to the house and rest all afternoon. Looks like you need a nap."

"Feels like it too." Elizabeth yawned again.

Still, she felt obligated to tidy up the shop before heading to the house. There were cobwebs in the far corner, and the floors needed to be swept.

Elizabeth had just retrieved the broom when she heard her ringtone. She set the broom aside and reached to pick up her cell phone from the counter. She answered with a hurried "Hello?"

"Elizabeth? It's John. I just wanted to see if you'd ever connected with Susanna."

"No, I wanted to go over there on my lunch break but never got a chance. I'll have to try again tomorrow. I'm exhausted." Elizabeth shifted her phone to her other ear and grabbed the broom. "I've been so busy chasing my tail that my follow-through is lousy." She did her best to start the process of sweeping, but nearly dropped the phone in the process.

"Chasing your tail?" John laughed. "Are we speaking figuratively, or is there an actual tail in this story?"

"There's a tail. A boxer's tail."

"Boxer, like in the ring, or boxer, the dog?"

"The dog." She stopped trying to sweep and set the broom aside.

"For the record, they have docked tails. And I'm still not sure what we're talking about."

Elizabeth did her best to get John caught up. She told him about her visit to Fred Zucker's house and then the phone call from Fred this morning.

"Well, first of all, I don't know how comfortable I am with the idea that you and Mary went off on this little adventure of yours by yourselves," he countered. "You went into a stranger's house alone? What if the man had been dangerous?"

She sighed and reached for the broom once again. "I know. Probably not our smartest move."

"You have to be careful. You just never know."

"I know, I know."

"Okay, well back to the point." John cleared his throat. "So let me see if I've got this—you've located the home of the man who owns the pitcher, but you don't know his current where-abouts, is that what you're saying?"

"Yes, and I'm worried about him. It doesn't make sense, I know. But I want to find him so we can settle up with him about the pitcher."

"And what do you make of the Wittmer name connection?" John asked.

"Probably just a coincidence. His neighbor seems to think he was always an Englischer."

"Hang tight for a couple of minutes. I'm going to do a search of our system and see if anyone has reported a Jackson Wittmer missing."

John disappeared for a few minutes, and Elizabeth decided to use the time sweeping up. She watched as Mary and Martha settled up the day's finances at the register. They were deep in conversation, probably about the wedding. Elizabeth found her mind wandering. By the time John returned on the line she'd finished sweeping and had put the broom away.

"No one has reported him missing."

"Strange." She stifled a yawn and fought the temptation to take a seat. If she sat down, she wouldn't feel like getting back up again. "I guess Fred hasn't had time yet. He told me he would call and make a report this afternoon."

"Look, as far as I know, Jackson Wittmer is comfortably resting on his sofa as we speak. Or maybe he's hanging out with a friend. Or he's gone to a movie."

"Only he's not." She flipped the switch to turn off the stockroom light. "He's definitely not at his house. And don't forget that he told Fred he was headed to the grocery store, but then he never returned. That's important."

"You mention this name Fred a lot."

"Right. Well, he's the only one who really knows anything." Elizabeth made her way up the aisle toward the front counter, where she found her sisters in some sort of debate about wedding decor. "Besides, the dog is with Fred. So are half of Jackson's belongings. He's been selling furniture and other items to Fred to make money."

"Mm-hmm." John's tone grew more serious. "I'm wondering if we should go over there and have a chat with Fred to see if he gives off any strange vibes."

"I can't leave right now, John. It's my night to make supper. Mary and Martha are both drowning in work for this wedding. Anna's getting married, you know."

"Not today, she's not," he countered. "The wedding's not till Saturday. I know, because I'm invited."

"Right." She lowered her voice and took a few steps away from her sisters, who were both still engrossed in their conversation. "But everyone's in a tizzy over the wedding preparations."

"Planning weddings is a lot more fun than chasing wannabe suspects, I guess." He chuckled. "Is that what you're saying?"

"No, actually. Just the opposite. Maybe I was born for sleuthing and not wedding planning. Definitely not my forte." She fought the temptation of a loud sigh.

"Elizabeth, I haven't known you long, but it's clear you're a good person. If I were you, I wouldn't worry too much about what other people are thinking. In fact, if I were you, I'd forget about tracking down Jackson Wittmer for a while."

"It's hard for my mind to let go of things."

"Then let me take it from here. I'll make a run to Jackson's house."

"You will?"

"Sure. And I'll talk to the neighbor too. I'll see if anything sounds suspicious. And I'll try to figure out why no missing-person report has been filed yet. How does that sound?"

"Comforting." She felt her shoulders slump forward. "I'm not saying Fred Zucker is suspect in any way, but he happens to be the closest person to Jackson at this time."

"We always look at neighbors, close friends, love interests, and spouses with a more critical eye. So trust me, my eyes are wide open."

"I'm glad someone's are." She yawned. "Going to bed early sounds really good, by the way."

"Great. Well, have a quick dinner, find a good book to read, and then crash."

"You've obviously never read a good book."

"What?"

"When you're reading a good book, you definitely don't fall asleep. You're up all night turning pages."

"Ah, good point. Well, find a boring book, then. Rest, Elizabeth. That's my point. I promise I won't let this slip through the cracks. I'll do what I can to track him down."

"Thank you, John. I'm grateful."

"Anytime."

She ended the call and discovered both sisters still at the register, talking about the wedding decor. Elizabeth joined them behind the counter where she snagged her purse and slung the strap over her shoulder.

"Ready to go?" Mary asked.

"Mm-hmm." Elizabeth yawned. "More than ready."

Now, if she could only stay awake long enough to cook dinner.

CHAPTER ELEVEN

Elizabeth had a hard time sleeping that night, but it had nothing to do with a book. She spent at least two hours tossing and turning in the bed, her thoughts a twisted mess. Her stomach was upset, but she couldn't figure out if she was genuinely ill or just worried and upset about the business with Jackson. As much as she tried to put him out of her mind, she could not. Something about the man—his story, his losses—had pierced her heart. She had to wonder if God hadn't used that pitcher to bring them together.

The pitcher.

She would call Susanna first thing tomorrow morning. If there was any chance Jackson was related to the Bird-in-Hand Wittmers, this whole story would begin to make sense. Perhaps, if she passed it off to the family, she could put these worries and concerns behind her.

Sometime around midnight Elizabeth rose from the bed and paced the room. She paused to pray—for Jackson, first of all. She couldn't even imagine what he must be going through, losing his child, his wife, his job, and now his home.

A rush of emotions settled over her as she pondered her life here at the farm and the store. It was not without its challenges. But there was a sense of security here. It made her physically ill to imagine what it would be like to lose it all. She didn't even want to think about the emotional devastation such losses would cause. Hopefully she would never have to.

As she walked toward the window and pulled back the curtain, Elizabeth thought about Job, the Bible character who lost so much in his life. Surely Jackson felt a bit like Job right about now. Was he, in spite of his struggles with alcohol, a man of faith? Was he leaning on God as he walked through these challenges? She couldn't really glean much from her conversation with Fred Zucker on that count.

Fred Zucker. He was an odd fellow, wasn't he? Kind of a loner, hanging out in that cluttered house of his. But he too made her sad. For what he had in possessions, he seemed to lack in people. How sad, to live your life surrounded by stuff but void of people. She paused to offer up a prayer for him, that he would somehow be able to replace things with people. He, like so many older people, needed relationships, friends.

Elizabeth stared out at the moon, a golden orb lighting the night sky. She was reminded of a poem her father had taught her as a child. *I see the moon and the moon sees me. God made the moon and God made me.* She thought of Jackson's daughter and wondered if Jackson had ever quoted that little poem to her.

To have a child for such a brief time and then to lose her... How could a parent ever truly get over such a thing?

Elizabeth's heart felt heavier than it had in ages. She began to pray in earnest, that God would bring healing to Jackson's heart and to Emily's too.

"Emily." She spoke his ex-wife's name aloud.

Emily Wittmer. How did she fit into all of this?

Elizabeth sat back down on her bed. "Why have You done this, Lord? Why have You brought this man into our lives?" There had to be some reason, far beyond an expensive porcelain pitcher. God was up to something here.

She finally fell into a fitful sleep where dreams about Rocky and Jackson consumed her, and she awoke with a headache the next morning. She just had one thing on her mind—caffeine. She walked down the stairs to the kitchen, where she found Martha wrapping freshly baked blueberry muffins to take to the shop.

"Good morning, sunshine." Martha smiled. "You slept late."

"I had trouble sleeping. Don't ask."

"Okay, I won't." Martha went back to work, humming a familiar song as she did.

Just as Elizabeth reached for her coffee mug, her cell phone rang. She pulled it from her pocket and noticed John's number. He sounded chipper with his opening "Good morning."

"Good morning." Elizabeth reached for her coffee mug again, ready to down the first cup. Hopefully it would squelch this headache.

"I have to ask the obvious question—did you stay up all night reading?"

"Not reading, but I did stay up most of the night. I just couldn't stop thinking about Jackson." She filled her mug with coffee and sat at the breakfast table.

"I told you to leave him to me, Elizabeth." A pause followed, and she could almost imagine John shaking his head. "I went by his house this morning before heading into the office."

"What did you find out?" She took a sip of her coffee and flinched. It was still hot.

"Well, for one thing, a representative from the bank was there, putting a notice on the garage door of the foreclosure."

"Oh no." This made Elizabeth even sadder than before. "Will he have a chance to go back in and get his things?"

"I was told that once that sign goes up, the locks are changed, and no one's allowed inside."

"Oh, how sad." She took another careful sip of her coffee.

"Yes. Maybe he can go in accompanied to get his things. I'm not sure how that works. The neighbor seemed pretty shaken up by it all."

"You met Fred?"

"Yeah. He seems like a nice enough old guy. Pretty crazy house, though."

"Right?" She reached over to snatch one of Martha's unwrapped muffins, then broke off a piece of it. "Did he explain why he hadn't filed the missing-person report?"

"Yes, and it made sense. He said he'd talked to the manager at a nearby gas station last night who claimed Jackson stopped by to purchase cigarettes and beer yesterday afternoon."

"Really?" She took a bite of the muffin and leaned back in her chair. "So there's been a sighting."

"There has. I stopped by the station and talked to him myself. He said Jackson looked awful, like he was really sick or something."

"Well, I'm sorry to hear that, but I'm relieved he's been spotted."

To her right, Martha reached for a napkin and set it down on the table in front of Elizabeth. She pointed to the muffin in Elizabeth's hand. Elizabeth took another bite of it before setting it down on the napkin.

"I knew you would be," John said. "The manager said Jackson looked pretty down on his luck, like a lot of the guys who hang out in that area."

"Yeah, I noticed that on the day we met. So where is this gas station, anyway?"

"Near Jaycee Park. Quite a few blocks from Jackson's house."

"So strange."

"Kind of a rough area. Lots of vagrants down that way. They frequent that station to buy beer."

"Did you go down there?"

"No. And I don't want you to, either. It's a rough area, as I said. But I've got a friend who works for Lancaster PD, and I'll ask him to keep an eye on the store for any sign of Jackson. Technically he's not a missing person until a report is filed. I mean, an adult is free to go wherever he likes unless there's a warrant out for his arrest or something like that. And there's not, by the way. I checked."

"Right." She grabbed her coffee mug and took a swallow, deep in thought over all of this.

"If there's no sign of foul play, we can't stop him from shifting from place to place. Lots of people do."

"True. But here's my concern—Jackson took off without telling his trusted friend, someone he usually confides in. He *said* he was coming back home, and yet he never showed up. So, even though he's been seen by someone in the area, even though he's not technically missing—from a legal standpoint, I mean—Fred is convinced something is amiss. I can't help but agree."

"Well, yes, but—"

"If Mary took off for the store and didn't return home at the expected time, I'd be worried sick. Sure, she's an adult. She's free to do as she pleases. But if she led me to believe she was going to do one thing then did another, I'd be worried. I'd be relieved to hear that someone else had spotted her, but if she didn't check in, I'd still consider her missing."

"Of course you would." He paused. "I do see your point. And if a couple more days go by without any more sightings, we'll fill out a missing-person report. Does that make you feel better?"

"Yes, thank you. I know Fred would appreciate it too."

John ended the call abruptly when another call came in on his end.

Elizabeth took another bite of her muffin and pondered the news she'd been given.

"Well?" Martha's brow wrinkled as she took the seat next to Elizabeth. "What did he have to say?"

"Jackson was spotted in Lancaster yesterday."

"That's good news."

"What did I miss?" Mary breezed into the kitchen and went straight for the coffeepot. "Something about Jackson?"

"He's been located," Martha said.

"Well, not exactly." Elizabeth fingered the handle of her mug. "He was seen making a purchase at a gas station yesterday."

"Has he gone back to his house?" Mary asked.

Elizabeth shook her head. "No, and that's another thing. John said that someone from the bank had come by to hang a foreclosure notice on the door."

"Sad." Mary filled her mug and took a seat across from Elizabeth.

"I know." She took another swig of her coffee. "So now I wonder if he's staying in a hotel somewhere in Lancaster. Or with a friend."

Mary reached for one of the muffins. "But surely he knows he could go to Fred's house. Don't you think?"

Elizabeth shrugged. "I'm clueless at this point. But please, don't let me get so distracted by all of this that I forget to call Susanna. I want to go by her place today to show her the pitcher and compare it with her washbasin."

The ladies ate their breakfast and then opened up the shop. Elizabeth was just about to ask her sisters if she could take a break and run to the Wittmer farm when Anna brushed in, all abuzz with excitement. Her hair was a bit of a mess, and her makeup looked a little wonky too. Judging from the bags under Anna's eyes, Elizabeth wasn't the only one who'd gone without sleep last night. Still, that didn't seem to bother Anna. She beamed with joy.

"Ladies, I can't believe the wedding is this weekend. I've hardly slept. I keep thinking about all the things that need to be done."

Mary rested her hand on Anna's arm. "Stop fretting, Anna. We've got this. And I don't know if I've said this yet or not, but I'm so grateful for the opportunity to help. I've always been the creative sort—painting and designing and so forth—and this has really helped me tap into my crafty side. I've had such a great time. Thanks for including me."

"You're welcome." Anna's cheeks turned crimson. "But I'm the lucky one. Not everyone is creative, so I'm blessed to have you on the team."

Elizabeth listened quietly as the ladies spoke. True, Mary was extremely creative and artistic. And Martha, of course, had a knack with baked goods. At times like these, Elizabeth wondered what she had to offer.

Anna forged ahead with her concerns. "You're the best, ladies, but I can't help thinking we're overlooking something. We have the decor. We have the food. Great call on having Capricios cater, Mary."

Mary nodded. "They're the best."

"Wayne and his brother are in charge of getting the tables, chairs, and tablecloths from the rental company. My family is doing the sweets and punch. And you ladies are working on centerpieces, decor, and cake. What else is there?"

"Silverware?" Mary asked. "Plates?"

"We're renting those too." Anna paused. "Would you believe Wayne's brother asked if we were having an open bar?" She shook her head. "He didn't take the news well, but he's still coming. Obviously. He's the best man."

The ladies carried on and on about the wedding. It was all Elizabeth could do not to interrupt them. Finally, when Anna paused for breath, Elizabeth managed to get their attention.

"I hate to ask," she said, "but could I leave for a half hour? I want to swing by Susanna's place with the pitcher."

Martha looked her way. "Sure, that would be fine."

"I won't be long, I promise." Elizabeth reached for her purse then headed to the stockroom to grab the pitcher. She was buzzing with excitement as she took the gorgeous antique into her arms. Within a matter of minutes she would know for sure if the pitcher and basin were a matched set. Elizabeth could hardly wait.

Mary kept an eye on the register while Martha and Anna chatted about wedding cakes. The shop saw a steady stream of customers, and many were in the mood to buy. Always a good thing. She stayed busy for nearly half an hour tending to customer after customer. One woman seemed particularly enamored with the antique furniture.

"I just love this shop," the woman said as she gestured to the handcrafted items. "It's my favorite in the area. So inviting. You ladies have done a fine job enticing us with all of these beautiful things."

"Thank you," Mary said, happy to hear such glowing praise. "We'd like to think so."

"I just love that little area you've created for the children to play in. What a sweet gesture. And wherever did you find that colorful alphabet rug? I'd love to get one just like it for my grandchildren."

"Oh, don't tell anyone, but we ordered it online." Mary laughed.

"I won't breathe a word. Now, I guess I'd better get busy shopping. We're on a time crunch today, but I couldn't resist swinging in. I need to fill up on jams and honey."

"We've got some wonderful maple syrup as well," Mary said. "Perfect for this season. We use maple in many of our baked goods during this time of year."

"Do you?" The woman's eyes widened. "I just use it on pancakes." She laughed heartily. Before long, she was browsing the aisles and filling a handheld basket with goodies. By the time Mary checked her out, the woman had purchased several hundred dollars' worth of items. Good news, indeed.

When the crowd thinned, Mary turned her attention to Martha and Anna. She was anxious to share an idea. "I've come up with the best plan ever. Why don't we do a ladies night out tonight? We can stop by Walmart for a last-minute shopping spree. I need to pick up ribbon for the centerpieces and white markers for the chalkboards. Then we can go to dinner. Your choice on the restaurant, Anna."

"I love that idea!" Anna pulled her hands to her chest, clearly excited. "After Saturday night, who knows how long it will be before I can hang out with my girlfriends. I'll be a newlywed." She giggled.

"Sounds good to me," Martha said. "I still need cake ingredients."

"I do hope Elizabeth will join us in the fun." Anna's smile curved down into a pout. "I should have asked for her input too, I suppose."

"She adores you," Mary explained. "But weddings aren't her thing."

"Really?" Anna looked perplexed by this notion. "But she's so organized and detail oriented. I would love to have her help too."

"Maybe you can tell her that when we're at dinner," Martha suggested. "It might boost her ego and make her feel included."

"Yes, I will." Anna's smile returned. "And in case I haven't said it before, I think you ladies are the best. I don't know why I didn't think to add you as bridesmaids…except that I've got too many already, what with all of my cousins and friends from work." She laughed. "Can you imagine someone at my age having eight bridesmaids, all younger than the bride?"

"I think it's sweet to be surrounded by friends and family like that," Mary said.

"And don't worry about not including me," Martha added. "I want to stay focused on the cake and the sweets."

"And you know I'll be up to my eyeballs in decorating until the very last minute," Mary said.

"Well, we were always such wonderful friends in our growing-up years." She smiled. "I miss those days. Life was much simpler back then."

"No going back," Mary said. "I wouldn't want to."

She was just about to add more to the conversation when the shop's phone rang. Mary answered it and was surprised to hear Elizabeth's voice on the other end.

"Well, that was a bust," her sister said. "Turns out Susanna and her brothers have gone out of town to accompany their aunt home. They won't be back until Friday morning."

"I'm so sorry, Lizzie," Mary said. "But I've come up with a great plan to get your mind off of things." She told her about the girls' night out, and before long Elizabeth sounded more chipper. Hopefully tonight they could all put their concerns aside and concentrate on just being friends and sisters.

CHAPTER TWELVE

After closing up the shop on Wednesday evening, Elizabeth decided to stop fretting over Jackson Wittmer and focus on Anna. Tonight was all about celebrating the bride-to-be, not solving mysteries or worrying about antique pitchers. Mary offered to drive, and all four ladies climbed into the SUV to head to dinner at El Ranchero, Anna's favorite Mexican restaurant.

Before long Mary was pulling into the parking lot of the superstore on Lincoln Highway. Anna agreed to shop with Martha for baking supplies while Elizabeth headed off to the craft department with Mary, who was searching for some last-minute bits of lace and burlap ribbon.

Before long, Elizabeth found herself completely swept into her sister's excitement. They moved from row to row, looking over the silk flowers, ribbons, and other decorative bits.

When they rounded the corner into the main aisle, Elizabeth felt Mary nudge her.

"Elizabeth, look." Mary discreetly pointed to a familiar young woman on the other end of the aisle. "Isn't that the mechanic from Chester's car lot?"

Elizabeth squinted to get a better look. Sure enough. Henrietta and another young woman had stopped their basket to look at a display of scrapbook items. "I think so. Same ponytail. Same double-pierced ear."

"Same navy-blue work shirt. It's her, all right. I can't get a good look at the other gal since she's turned sideways, but that's Henrietta, for sure." Mary put a finger to her lips and turned the cart to follow Henri and her friend, who maneuvered their way down the school supplies aisle. They were apparently in a hurry to get somewhere. Mary tailed them every step of the way.

By the time they reached the health and beauty department, Elizabeth was fed up…and tired. She froze in place and put her hands on her hips. "Enough already, Mary. I refuse to follow two innocent shoppers from department to department. This is just silly. And intrusive."

"Aren't you at all curious about that guy from Chester's Autos?" Mary eased her cart past an elderly man who was looking at antacids. "Henrietta works with him. She might drop a few clues if we stick close."

"The only thing she's liable to drop is that jumbo-sized box of antacids she's picking up," Elizabeth countered in a hoarse whisper. "And keep your voice down, will you? This is already awkward enough without her seeing us."

They stood and watched while Henrietta tossed the antacids into her basket, then took a few steps toward the vitamin aisle, chatting with her friend all the while.

Mary nudged her basket along in an attempt to keep up. She tossed several antacids into their basket as well. "I say we go over there and talk to her."

"We're here to shop for wedding decor, not quiz almost-complete strangers," Elizabeth responded. "Besides, what would we ask her?"

"If Chester is really up to no good, as Fred Zucker seems to think, maybe Henri's in on it. I say we offer a how-do-you-do and engage her in conversation. What could it hurt?"

"I don't know, Mary. I mean, we're supposed to be meeting Anna and Martha on the baking aisle. Don't you think they'll get irritated if we keep them waiting? And she's not alone, anyway. She's got a friend with her." Elizabeth watched as the other woman knelt down to look at something on the bottom row of the vitamin aisle. Something about the blond seemed familiar, but she couldn't quite put her finger on it. "It's just awkward."

"It's only as awkward as we make it. Come on." Mary bolted down the vitamin aisle until she ended up with her buggy bumping into Henri's. Literally.

"Oh, excuse me, I—" Mary waved her hand in the air. Elizabeth just wanted to crawl into a hole. Or run.

Henri looked their way, and her eyes widened. "Well, hey."

"Fancy bumping into you here." Mary flashed a broad smile. "We're shopping for wedding cake ingredients. What are you looking for?"

Henri laughed. "Before I tell you, I should probably clue you in that you're in the pharmacy department, not on the baking aisle. I don't think you're going to find any wedding cake ingredients here."

"Oh, I know." Mary reached over and grabbed a bottle of vitamin C tablets and set them in her cart. "One can never have too many vitamins." She paused and gazed intently at Henri. "So, how are things going at Chester's?"

"Oh, pretty good. I've been working on an older-model Fiat that came in this morning. Nice car, but there are problems with the starter and ignition switch. I'm taking care of those before we get it on the lot."

She carried on about the vehicle's problems, but Elizabeth found herself completely distracted as Henri's friend rose from her squatting position and faced them head on. Elizabeth's breath caught in her throat as she realized she was looking directly into the eyes of Emily Wittmer, Jackson's ex-wife.

"Where do you think they are, Martha?"

"What?" Martha looked up from the shopping cart and noticed the worry lines creasing Anna's brow.

"Your sisters. Where do you suppose they are? I've got family coming in tonight after our dinner, and I don't want to miss them. If I'd realized the shopping excursion was going to take this long, I probably would've said no to coming with you gals."

"I'm so sorry, Anna." Martha glanced at the clock on her phone. "It's been twenty minutes since we split up. They said they'd meet us in ten minutes. I'll call Mary. I'm sure she just got distracted in the craft department. And I distinctly remember her saying something about needing burlap ribbon, so she's probably lost in her creativity. You know how she is." Martha pulled up Mary's name on her phone and pushed the button.

Seconds later, her sister answered with a rushed, "I'm sorry. We're on our way." Just as quickly, the call ended.

"I think they must be close." Martha offered a strained smile. "And I think we've got everything we need for the cake—flour, sugar, eggs, butter, baking powder." She glanced up and saw the confectioner's sugar. "Oh!" She grabbed several bags. "I can't believe I almost forgot this. We'll need plenty for the icing."

"Not sure I want icing," Anna said. "I've been thinking about going naked."

"Excuse me?" Martha almost choked at this news.

Anna laughed. "I mean, I've been thinking about having a naked cake."

"Naked cake?" This was surprising.

Her friend's eyes lit in excitement, and she clasped her hands together. "Yes, and I promise, this is the last time I'm going to change my mind. Wayne and I are both in agreement—the cake needs to be simple. Plain. Maybe add some fall leaves and greenery. Maybe some blackberries and strawberries… something like that. You've seen naked cakes before, right?"

Martha nodded, and a wave of relief washed over her. This would be a simple project, after all. "Well, yes, we skimmed past a few while looking at pictures of wedding cakes the other day. But when we spoke last you had changed your mind from the white cake with black piping to a cake that looked like a birch tree. Remember?"

"I know, I know. But I stayed up half the night last night looking at pictures, and the birch tree idea just didn't settle well with me."

"I see." Martha paused to listen to Anna's passionate discourse about how trendy naked cakes were at the moment. She didn't interject for fear Anna would change her mind…again.

"So let me see if I understand this," Martha said. "You want a cake that looks like most of the frosting has been scraped off."

"Exactly." Anna sighed. "I do. I can send you pictures if you like."

"No, no, that's okay. I can look at the pictures we found before and also look them up online to make sure I've got the right idea. But before I do, I want to make absolutely sure this is what you want. I can't add frosting to it at the last minute, and piping or other details will be completely out of the question." She hated to mention it, but naked cakes had one major downfall. Unlike other, more traditional cakes, there was no way to cover any flaws. Every layer had to be baked to the exact same color and leveled perfectly.

"I'm absolutely sure. This is what I want."

"Okay, then. One naked wedding cake, coming up."

"I'm sorry," Elizabeth said as she and Mary came to a stop beside the other ladies on the baking aisle. "Did I just hear you use the words *naked* and *wedding* in the same sentence?"

Martha nodded. "You did. Anna has decided she wants a—"

"Naked cake." Elizabeth spoke in tandem with her sister. "I heard. So that's a real thing?"

"Absolutely." Anna's eyes filled with excitement. "They're all the rage right now."

"It's basically a cake without icing," Martha explained. "Though there's a thin layer of icing that gets scraped away. It leaves just enough of a residue to keep the outer edges of the cake from drying out."

"Sounds very...plain," Elizabeth said.

"Which, if you think about it, is perfect for a rustic wedding in the Amish country." Mary shrugged.

"I don't know why I didn't think of this earlier." Anna beamed with excitement. "All of the brides are having them. And it's perfect for those folks who aren't keen on too much icing."

"People like that exist?" Mary looked stunned.

"Who knew?" Elizabeth laughed. "Well, I know one thing for sure—if I ever do get married, you're making my cake, Martha. But I want you to clothe it properly."

"Oh?" Martha raised her eyebrows.

"Yes. In fact, you can coat it in cream cheese icing, pecans, and coconut. Italian cream cake is my favorite, you know."

"Speaking of food, are we about ready to get out of here?" Mary asked. "My stomach's been rumbling nonstop."

"Well, it looks like you've got enough antacids to solve that problem." Anna gazed down into their cart and her eyes widened. "Didn't know you had stomach troubles, Mary."

Mary glanced down into her cart. "Only on occasion. Guess I'd better put most of these back on the shelf. Anyway, let's go eat dinner. I'm dying for some enchiladas, and El Ranchero is the best."

"Mm-hmm." Anna seemed to lose herself to her thoughts. "I just love their chips and salsa. And their green sauce is delicious."

"I thought you were off carbs," Martha said. "Isn't that what you said?"

"With only four days till the wedding? I'd say it's time to stop worrying about all of that. Besides, if Wayne doesn't love me as I am, he's picked the wrong woman. And I'd say it's a little late for him to swap me out for someone new."

They walked to the front of the store, paid for their items, and then got in the SUV. Elizabeth wanted to tell Martha all about running into Henri and Emily but didn't want to interrupt Anna, who carried on and on about the wedding reception, which was now the focus of the conversation. Mary took her place behind the wheel and pointed the SUV in the direction of El Ranchero.

When they got to the corner of Rutledge, Elizabeth happened to notice a gas station. Her conversation with John came back to her, and it was all she could do not to squeal aloud. "Mary, could you stop at this gas station for a minute?"

"What? Why?" Mary tapped the brakes and slowed the car.

"Let's top off the tank with gas."

"Here?" The pitch of Mary's voice rose a notch. "No way. Not in this part of town. Besides, we've still got a third of a tank."

"Please, Mary. Just pull in. I'll explain in a minute."

"Okay, but I'm holding you personally responsible if anything happens."

This, of course, caused Anna to go into a panic. "I can't afford for anything to happen, ladies. This is not a good week for a catastrophe of some sort. I do hope you haven't got something up your sleeve, Elizabeth."

"I'm just getting gas." Elizabeth got out of the car. "I'll pay inside," she said before closing the door. "Be right back."

Martha bounded from the car, a scowl on her face. "Not alone, you won't. I don't know what you're up to, but you're not doing it by yourself."

They walked into the store, and Elizabeth caught a whiff of the man in front of them, an older gentleman in dirty clothes with a case of beer under his arm. He shifted the beer to his other arm and complained about the long line of customers ahead of him.

By the time Elizabeth and Martha got up to the register, she'd almost lost the courage to talk to the clerk. He seemed pretty impatient. So did the customers behind her.

"I need twenty dollars at pump three." She handed him her card. While the purchase ran, she eased her way into the conversation. "Say, I was just wondering if you'd seen a friend of mine. He's been missing a few days. Thirty-something. Dark hair. Tanned."

"Same guy the police were looking for when they stopped by yesterday?" The cashier quirked a bushy brow.

Elizabeth nodded and then signed the ticket he placed in front of her. "Yes."

"Look, I told the officer the same thing I'll tell you...he came, he went. People come and go all the time. You see this line of customers? Soda. Cigarettes. Beer. Gas. That's what I sell. I run a busy store. I don't go getting in people's business, and they don't go getting in mine. Got it?"

"Got it. But, just for the record, you haven't seen him again today, have you?"

"No."

"Lady, is this gonna take all night?" the man behind her grumbled. "I've got someplace I need to be."

"Sorry!' She reached into her purse for a business card, which she gave to the clerk. "If you happen to see him, will you please call this number? There are plenty of people worried about him, that's all."

The man took the card with a grunt and then turned his attention to the customer behind her.

"What was all that about?" Martha mumbled as they walked toward the door.

"When I realized this was the same gas station where Jackson was spotted, I couldn't resist. John said the clerk said Jackson was here yesterday, so I was kind of hoping he knew a little more about him or where he is."

"And what would we do if we found out where he is?" Martha put her hands on her hips. "The man has lost his wife, his child, his home, his truck. The last thing he needs is two strangers getting in his business."

"At first I wanted to find him to let him know the pitcher is worth more than we thought. At this point I'm just worried about him because the clerk said he looked really sick. And by the way, now that I have you alone, I should tell you that we ran into Jackson's ex-wife in Walmart just now."

"What? Are you sure?"

"Very. Henri introduced her by name."

"Who's Henri?"

"You know, the mechanic that Mary and I told you about. She works at Chester's Autos."

Martha put her hand up in the air. "Let me get this straight. The mechanic from the auto shop is friends with Jackson's ex-wife?"

"Yes. Now you're catching on. Something is rotten in Denmark."

"And in Lancaster County," Martha quipped. "But can I ask a favor? Could we just pump the gas, go to El Ranchero, and eat some chips and salsa? Right now that's about all I can handle. And I'm pretty sure Anna's in the car having a meltdown because we're taking so much time. That overactive imagination of hers has probably convinced her she's about to get robbed. Or worse. So can we get this show on the road?"

"Of course."

Martha led the way out of the front door of the station, and Elizabeth tagged along behind her. She walked past the newspaper bin and happened to glance down as the photo of a familiar man caught her eye.

Chester O'Conner.

Just above the photo, the headline stood out in bold font. Elizabeth's breath caught in her throat as she read the words: LOCAL CAR DEALER FACING POSSIBLE FRAUD CHARGES.

CHAPTER THIRTEEN

Elizabeth pulled back the covers and settled beneath them, hoping she could sleep. After snapping off the lamp, she rested her head on the pillow. Just as she started to fall asleep, the image of that newspaper headline jumped out at her once again, bringing her fully awake.

Local Car Dealer Facing Possible Fraud Charges

Chester O'Conner.

Fraud.

Was he really capable of such a thing? If so, did his evil impulses go beyond that to deeper crimes? Had he done something to Jackson, perhaps? Something sinister? Was that why he wanted the truck so badly, to get to its owner?

Her imagination kicked into overdrive. She pictured Jackson arriving at the car lot, then saw him responding unfavorably to Chester's wheeling and dealing. She saw him walking away from the deal, then imagined Chester coming after him, ready to…she wasn't sure what. Her imagination didn't take her that far.

"Stop it, Elizabeth," she chided herself as a yawn escaped. "You're making mountains out of molehills, just like Anna does. Don't let your imagination run away with you."

She rested her eyes and prayed for her sisters and their children and grandchildren, then turned her prayers to

Jackson and his ex-wife. Before long, she dozed off. What seemed like minutes later she awoke, riddled with questions. Her mind simply wouldn't rest. It was like a movie reel that just kept going and going. Perhaps the movie wouldn't stop until she knew Jackson was safe and sound.

Elizabeth really needed time alone with Mary and Martha to discuss the encounter with Henri and Emily. It did seem strange that the two women were friends. More than a coincidence, anyway. Had Emily somehow cooked up a plot so she could end up with the house?

No, that made no sense. The house was already in foreclosure, right? What other motives could she have? And why involve the folks at Chester's Autos?

After thinking it through a bit, Elizabeth finally shook off her questions. No point in getting worked up over speculation. What she needed—what they all needed—was proof that something was amiss at Chester's Autos.

After a quick breakfast, she headed to the shop ahead of her two sisters. Before the doors opened to the public, she wanted to spend some time doing research.

Mary buzzed through the front door, chattering about the weather, completely oblivious to the work Elizabeth was doing on the laptop. She carried on and on about the leaves that had fallen and how beautiful the farm looked covered in reds, golds, and oranges. Then she disappeared down the center aisle toward the stockroom at the back.

When Martha entered the shop a few minutes behind her, she gave Elizabeth a puzzled look. "You were up early this morning, Lizzie. What was the rush?"

"Just had something on my mind. Decided to do a little research."

"Oh?" This seemed to get Martha's attention. She set her purse down and walked behind the counter. "Tell me."

Elizabeth enlarged the photo on her screen and turned it to face her sister. "I'm on the Better Business Bureau site. Look at all these complaints against Chester's Autos. There are dozens of them. It's kind of shocking that he's still in business, really. I would think they'd shut him down over all this."

"Fraud?" Martha's eyes widened. "Really?"

"Yes. I didn't get a chance to tell you last night, because I wanted to keep things light around Anna, but I saw a newspaper headline about Chester. Apparently he's been accused of fraud."

"Whoa."

"Yes. And from what I've gathered from my online snooping, there are lots of shady dealings going on over there— everything from changing out VIN numbers to hiring repo guys to take back cars from folks who got behind on payments."

"Repos aren't unusual," Martha said. "They happen all the time."

"Well, some of the stories are pretty extreme," Elizabeth countered. "And that's not all. One man said he brought his car in to be appraised, and Chester asked for the keys. He passed them—and the car—off to his mechanic, and then got busy trying to sell the guy a new vehicle. When the man said he wasn't there to buy—only to sell—his car keys mysteriously went missing. The customer felt duped. He thought Chester was trying to keep him there longer so he could keep up his sales pitch. Poor guy felt trapped."

"So do you think Henrietta is in cahoots with Chester, then?"

"That's what has me so troubled this morning. She seems like such a nice young woman. And she's apparently good friends with Emily, based on what we saw last night at the store."

"Right. But what does any of this have to do with Jackson Wittmer?" Martha sighed. "Sorry, none of this is making sense to me. Just because Chester is up to no good doesn't mean he's responsible for anything outside of the car lot."

"Maybe. Or maybe not."

"But how does this implicate him in Jackson's case?" Martha asked. "Jackson was just there to sell his truck. And he sold his truck. End of story. Right?"

"Maybe." Elizabeth closed the laptop as their first customer arrived at the front door. She lowered her voice to share the rest of her thoughts. "I'm just curious about why Jackson would leave home and not return again on the very same day he sold his truck. If Chester has a history of fraud I think we'd be foolish not to consider the notion that he might be behind Jackson's disappearance. He wanted the man's truck, that much we know for sure. But why?"

"Fraud and kidnapping are two completely different things. Even if Chester's as bad as the paper implies, that hardly makes him a kidnapper."

"I wouldn't be so sure. And if Chester's involved, we can't help but link the mechanic and the ex-wife to the story as well. It could be we're looking at a whole ring of bad guys here, Martha. Think about that."

"All I'm thinking right now is that you have an overactive imagination, Elizabeth." Martha turned her attention to greeting the customer, offering a hearty, "Welcome to Secondhand Blessings. Let us know if we can help you with anything." She then turned back to Elizabeth. "Be careful not to let yourself get too caught up in this, okay? We need to stay focused today. It's Thursday. Quilt guild. Rachel will be here soon."

"Right. I'll try. I'm just worried about Jackson. There's got to be some reason the Lord led him to us, some reason why we're caught up in this story at all. You know? I don't think his visit here was a mistake or an accident. I think God is trying to use us in some way to help him." In fact, she felt sure of it.

"I suppose that's possible. But God wouldn't want us to get in over our heads, would He?"

"I suppose not." Elizabeth paused. "Still, I say we go back to Chester's Autos as soon as we close up shop this afternoon. There are questions left unanswered, and I'm not going to rest until we've turned over every rock."

"Go back?" Martha shook her head. "Let me pray about that. I'm not as convinced. And I'm pretty sure John wouldn't be either."

Martha headed off to help their customer and Elizabeth pondered her sister's words. She had a point. Elizabeth did have an overactive imagination. And it might not make much sense to go back over to Chester's place, especially if he was as shady as the papers and the internet implied. She certainly didn't want to put her sisters in any danger. Or herself either, for that matter.

Elizabeth didn't have time to ponder the what-ifs much longer because John entered the store a few minutes later. He caught her eye and waved at her before walking her way. Before she could even say a word about last night's adventures, his smile shifted into a frown.

John crossed his arms at his chest and gave her a pensive look. "Tell me you did not go into that gas station last night, Elizabeth."

"Well, I…"

"She went in," Martha called out from down the aisle.

"I called the manager this morning to check in, and he said that a woman matching your description came in last night asking a bunch of questions."

"Not a *bunch* of questions," she argued. "I just wondered if he'd seen Jackson again after that first sighting, that's all."

"And if he had?" John's eyes narrowed to slits. "Then what?"

"I don't know." She released a loud sigh. "It might have eased my mind?"

"Did it ever occur to you that easing your mind might be adding stress to mine?" John shook his head. "I told you not to go anywhere near that place. It's in a rough part of town."

"It's not like we planned it. We literally just happened by it on our way to the restaurant for dinner. I couldn't help myself, John. Seriously."

"Sure you couldn't."

"No, I mean it." Her voice grew more animated as she attempted to explain. "There it was, like a light beckoning. I had to go inside to check the place out. I was really hoping I'd learn something."

"And you learned…what?"

She shrugged. "That people at that time of night are very impatient when they're standing in line at a gas station. And that a lot of people buy cigarettes and beer from gas stations. Anyway, I gave the owner—or the clerk, whoever he was—my card. That way he can call me if he sees Jackson."

"He has your personal information?" Now John's voice bordered on panic.

"Yes." Elizabeth swallowed hard. "Is that bad?"

"He has your address, your phone number, and your email. But other than that, I'd say it was a perfectly safe move." John's words now carried a sarcastic ring.

"Oh." She released a slow sigh. Okay, so maybe it hadn't been her smartest move. Had she put the shop—or her sisters— in danger? She sure hoped not. "He seemed like a nice enough guy. Besides, I don't think he's ever going to look at my card again, if you want the truth of it. He just shoved it into his pocket and waited on his next customer. You know? I was nothing but a nuisance to him. He made that perfectly obvious."

"Well, that's hopeful." The wrinkles in John's forehead relaxed a bit. "You can never be too careful, Elizabeth. I know you ladies have had a few adventures lately. Your sleuthing skills are impressive. But that doesn't mean you need to be risking your lives, especially for people you barely know. And let's be honest, you barely know this Jackson guy. Right?"

"Right. And yes, I hear you loud and clear."

"Good. I wanted to let you know that I have Jackson Wittmer's phone number and have been trying to call him. It's going straight to voice mail. The phone must be shut off, because we're not able to track it to a location."

"That's too bad."

"Yes. But I'm still looking for him. I just wanted you to know."

"Thank you, John. I can't help but wonder if he's safe out there. I hear we have a big storm blowing in tonight. That concerns me."

"Yeah, it's gonna be a doozie. Hope it doesn't put a damper on Anna's wedding." He laughed. "Get it? Storm? Damper?"

She groaned at his pun and then paused to listen to his rich, warm laugh. Something about John always brought a smile to her face...when he wasn't scolding her, anyway. He had a great sense of humor, for sure.

He spent a few more minutes in the shop and then had to take a call. Mary joined Elizabeth at the register. "What was that about?"

"He found out I went into the gas station last night and decided I needed a little reprimanding."

"Ack." Mary's nose wrinkled. "Well, I knew it wasn't a good idea, but what could I do? I was stuck in the car with Anna. She was panicking, by the way. She felt sure we were going to get robbed or something like that, three days before her big day. You wouldn't believe all the scenarios she played out in her head while you were in there."

"That's what we figured. I know how active her imagination is. But I was only inside for five minutes, Mary."

"Seemed more like fifty-five, what with Anna fretting the whole time. But I'm sure you're right."

"I am. And we were perfectly safe in the store." Still, even as Elizabeth said the words, she didn't fully believe them. Any number of things could have gone wrong last night. Thank goodness the situation had ended well.

She did her best to focus on customers and quilt guild ladies. Martha seemed more than a little out of sorts today. She was wound up in knots over the incoming storm, afraid it might interfere with her cake baking. She planned to start the cakes tonight but seemed overly anxious about it all. Every time there was a lull in the crowd, she would come back up to the register to share more of her concerns. Before long, Elizabeth was nervous for her. Putting together a four-tiered cake—even a naked one—was apparently a bit more than Martha could take from a psychological standpoint. When they reached closing time Martha didn't even stick around to help close up. Instead, she begged off and headed straight to the house to get busy on the cake.

As she swept up, Elizabeth couldn't stop thinking about the visit from John. She didn't really blame him for worrying, but why did he have to come on so strong? Elizabeth wasn't prone to impulsive decisions, after all.

Like the one brewing right now.

Elizabeth's thoughts were riveted to Chester O'Conner and to that headline. The man was facing possible fraud charges. She felt in her gut that one more visit to Chester's Autos was in order. Now that she knew of Henri's connection to Emily Wittmer and Chester's ties to crime, she might be more inclined to ask the right questions or discover hidden truths.

After she finished her sweeping, Elizabeth shared her idea with Mary, who didn't receive it well at all.

"Go back to Lancaster...this evening?" Mary shook her head. "No thanks."

"But I don't want to go alone, Mary. I was really hoping you would—"

"Oh, trust me, you're not going alone. I won't allow that."

"Then come with me. I promise it'll be the last time. I mean, I hope it will be." She gave her sister a pleading look.

"What are we looking for, specifically?" Mary asked. "I mean, it's not like they're hiding Jackson there, at a used-car dealership."

"I don't know what we're looking for, but I'll know it if we find it." Elizabeth shrugged. "Come on. I think we need to follow our guts."

"*Your* gut," Mary countered. "There are a thousand other things I'd rather do than go back to Chester's Autos. Have I mentioned that I'm helping with Anna's wedding? I have to work on the chalkboards tonight and make the bows for the church pews. Not to mentioning repairing one of the centerpieces that fell apart. I've got a lot to do, Lizzie."

"It won't take long, I promise."

After a moment, Mary nodded. "Okay, I'll go back on one condition."

"What's what?" Elizabeth asked.

"If you'll call John and ask him to meet us there."

Elizabeth shrugged. "That's not a bad idea." She reached for her phone and punched in his number. He didn't answer, so she left a message. Hopefully he would get it before too long and join them in Lancaster, where they would put an end to this crazy story once and for all.

CHAPTER FOURTEEN

Mary could have kicked herself. How she let her sister talk her into driving back to Lancaster this evening, when she had so much to do, was beyond her. She should have been working on wedding decor, not solving crimes. Still, how could she turn Elizabeth down when she seemed fueled by such passion? Finding out what had happened to Jackson Wittmer had become a driving force in her sister's life. Strange, considering the fact that they didn't even know the man. It wasn't like Elizabeth to get this wound up in someone else's story.

Unless she felt the Lord's prompting.

Mary couldn't get past the notion that her sister probably was following the Lord's lead. So she'd better play along.

The drive seemed to take longer than usual. Perhaps that had something to do with her anxiety, which was through the roof. She pulled the SUV into the lot at Chester's Autos and groaned as the owner walked their way. Before she could say, "Now, Lizzie, please be careful," her sister had bounded from the passenger seat and was standing next to Chester O'Conner. So much for Elizabeth being the shy, unassuming one.

Mary climbed out of the car just in time to hear Chester's opening question. "Ladies, have you come back to buy that truck? I told you it was a deal you couldn't pass up. Well, you're in luck. It's still here and at a truly great price too."

"Buy the truck?" Mary looked across the lot and noticed the red Ford still in the same spot. She couldn't help but notice that the price had been lowered to $16,999. Interesting. If they held out long enough, Chester might end up giving them that truck.

"I know you had your eye on it." Chester rubbed his hands together. "If you like, I can have my appraiser look over your SUV while you're waiting. I'm sure I can give you a fair trade-in. Chester lives to please."

"No, we're definitely not here to buy." These words came from Elizabeth, who seemed bolder than usual. "Just here to ask a few questions."

For a moment Chester looked disappointed. But just as quickly, his frown morphed back into a smile. "Fire away. I'm still convinced you're here for the truck though. Maybe you just don't know it yet. That's often the case with my customers. But I'll be happy to answer your questions, ladies...anything for a sale."

"Funny you should say that, since my questions will take us in that direction." Elizabeth reached into her purse and pulled out her notepad and pen. Wow, she really was taking all of this seriously. "First of all, I read the article in the paper."

Chester's confidence appeared to waver. "Wait a minute, wait a minute. That's why you're here, because of that bogus article? Ladies, I might be skilled in the art of negotiation, but that doesn't make me a crook, despite what you read to the contrary." He gestured to the cars in the lot. "You'll notice the shop is still open. They haven't shut me down."

"Yet," Elizabeth said.

"There's no *yet*. It's not going to happen, I tell ya. Now, if I was really a swindler and cheat, wouldn't they have made me close up shop already? Wouldn't I be sitting in a jail cell right now?" He shook his head. "No, the whole thing was just a big misunderstanding. I'm sure I can clear it up if you want to come into my office. How does a nice cup of coffee sound?" He rubbed his hands together. "It's a little chilly out here, so I could use something hot myself."

"No coffee, thanks." Elizabeth clicked her pen and scribbled something in her notebook.

Chester looked around, as if trying to figure out who might be watching them. Was he nervous?

Mary decided to put him at ease. This whole thing could blow up in a hurry if he got frantic. "We won't take much of your time, Mr. O'Conner," she said. "In fact, we need to get back home pretty quickly. But I believe Elizabeth has a few questions about Jackson."

"Jackson?" Now Chester really looked nervous. "No word on him yet?"

"He was spotted at a local gas station a couple of days ago, but not since." Elizabeth jotted down a note and then looked up. "I'm starting to get worried."

"I understand. I'm concerned about that news myself."

"I'm trying to retrace his steps in the hopes that it will give us some clues about where he's gone. So, if you don't mind, I'd like to have more details about the day he was here."

Creases formed between Chester's brows. "I told you, he came and went a few times but finally showed up on Saturday, ready to sell. I made him a deal. He got his things out of the truck, then left."

"And since then?"

"Since then...what?" Chester looked genuinely perplexed. "I haven't seen him at all. I told you I drove out to his place, but he wasn't there. Remember? I did that as a favor to you, by the way, because you were worried." Chester tugged at his collar. "And to put my own mind at ease, I suppose. I was concerned about the guy. Still am. But I don't know him well enough to speculate about where he might be."

Elizabeth didn't respond, but she wrote something down in her notepad.

Mary decided to interject a quick, "Thank you for making the drive to Jackson's place," to calm Chester down. The poor guy looked like he was about to pop a cork. "We are grateful you were willing to do that."

"Well then, what are you implying with all of these questions?" he asked. "Do you think I had something to do with Jackson's disappearance? If so, you can take those accusations and be on your way. I would never hurt anyone, especially not a customer."

"No accusations here, Mr. O'Conner," Mary said.

"Well, good." His shoulders slumped. "Because that's all I need right now, more accusations. I've got enough on my plate as it is. So trust me when I say that my dealings with Jackson were completely aboveboard. If you don't believe me, talk to Henri again. She'll vouch for me. She was here through the whole thing. And she knows me better than anyone here, I suppose."

Before she could respond, Mary's cell phone started ringing. She reached into her purse, fished it out, and looked at the name on the screen. Anna. Great. Talk about awkward timing. Time to switch to wedding-planning gear once again.

Mary stepped aside to answer several questions from the bride-to-be, most of them about the weather. It looked like they might need a Plan B for tomorrow's prep day, if this incoming storm was really going to be as bad as everyone said. Judging from the gray skies overhead, Anna was right to worry.

Elizabeth tried to keep up the conversation with Chester while Mary was on the phone, but his attentions had shifted to an incoming customer. As he took off across the parking lot, her gaze turned to the skies, which were darkening above. It looked like they were in for a doozie of a storm. She and Mary should probably get home before a downpour started.

Before she could give the idea much thought, Elizabeth caught a glimpse of Henrietta walking toward them. The young woman's eyes lit up the moment she saw them.

"Hey, we meet again." The young woman offered a bright smile and then wagged her finger in the air. "If I didn't know any better, I'd say you were following me."

Elizabeth swallowed hard. "No, I, um…it was just a coincidence that we saw you in the store last night. And we're here today to try to get some answers to questions."

"Questions?"

"Yes. We're looking for more details about the day the owner of that red truck took off."

"Took off?" Henri looked perplexed.

"Yes, the same day he sold the truck to Chester, he went to the grocery store but never returned home."

"That's awful. Why didn't you say something last night?"

"Well, you were with a friend." Elizabeth watched to see how Henri would respond to this line. If she and Emily had something to do with Jackson's disappearance, maybe her expression would give her away.

Nothing.

"Anyway..." Elizabeth leaned against the truck and gave Henri a closer look. "He was spotted at a gas station a few days later, but the manager said he looked really ill, so we're concerned about his well-being."

"Obviously."

"We decided to come back and ask Chester a few questions. And after reading the article in the paper about him, I couldn't help but wonder if he might have something to do with, well..."

"Wait." Henri put her hands up. "Are you saying you think Chester had something to do with that man's disappearance? And you're basing those speculations on that stupid article in the paper?"

"I'm not sure. But that's why I'm here, to get some answers."

"You're definitely barking up the wrong tree. I can tell you that right now. He had nothing to do with any of that, I can assure you." Henri released a nervous laugh, but Elizabeth could tell she wanted this conversation to come to a close.

Elizabeth gave the young woman a pensive look. "Can I ask you a question?"

"Sure." Henri leaned against the truck and squinted against the setting sun. "I'm an open book."

"Why keep working for Chester if there's a chance those speculations are true?"

Henri's gaze shifted to Chester, who was speaking with a customer a few yards away. "He's slick," she said. "Some would just say he skates on the edge of slimy. But he's not a bad man. There's no way I would keep working for him if I really believed that. I've known him since I was a kid. He's one of my dad's best friends. Trust me when I say I would've quit my job if I really thought he was guilty of something illegal."

"According to the paper, he committed fraud."

Henri's jaw flinched. "No...according to the paper, police are *considering* filing fraud charges. There's a difference. Don't you think they would've already done so if they really had the evidence to convict him?"

"Maybe...or maybe not."

"Look, where I come from a person is innocent until proven guilty." Henri paced back and forth and then came to a stop. She looked Elizabeth in the eye. "I know things look bad, but I also know Chester. Most of this brouhaha originated from one customer who wasn't happy with the vehicle Chester sold him. I was in the room when the guy came barreling in with his lawyer, demanding justice because the car broke down a week after he paid cash for it. I heard Chester offer the guy his money back and even agree to trade in the vehicle he'd sold him for something else at no additional cost. But it wasn't enough for the guy. He was angry and wanted vengeance. He started tracking down other customers and getting them stirred up."

"Really?" Elizabeth jotted down this information.

"Yes, and he convinced quite a few to file complaints with the Better Business Bureau. Then he went to the police. Concocted a story that was a variation of the truth, with just enough accusations in it to make the police suspicious. Chester was hard-hit on multiple sides at once. I can tell you, having witnessed it firsthand, that it took a toll on him. And the newspaper article has been like a knife in the chest, not just for him, but all of us who work for him."

"Hmm." Elizabeth wasn't so sure she believed all of that. "So let me ask you a question. When I stopped by a couple of days back and asked you about the owner of that red Ford F-150, you seemed to know who Jackson was."

"Sure." Henri shrugged. "I'd just seen him. He came back to get something out of the glove box. I think I told you about that. Remember?"

"Yes, but I'm guessing you knew about him long before that day, right?"

"Long before that day?" Henrietta looked genuinely perplexed. "I saw him come by a time or two to see what Chester would offer him for the truck, but I never knew him. Still don't, for that matter."

"But you seem to be pretty close friends with his wife. Er, ex-wife."

"I...*what?*" Now Henri looked more confused than ever.

"Emily Wittmer," Elizabeth said. "You were shopping with her in Walmart last night."

Henri's eyes bugged. "Hang on. You're saying that Em used to be married...to Jackson? The same guy we're talking about?"

"Of course. I assumed you knew all of that."

Henri shook her head and stepped away from the truck. "Look, here's the deal—I just met Em at a Bible study a couple of weeks back. I knew she was divorced, but we never discussed any particulars about her ex, at least not by name. I just knew her as a woman with a broken heart who'd lost a baby and a husband, nothing more. Certainly never put it together that she was in any way connected to that red truck." Henri's eyes narrowed. "Are you sure about all this?"

"Very sure."

Henri grew quiet for a moment and appeared to be thinking. After a second she put her hand over her mouth, then pulled it away. "Oh my goodness. Remember how I told you that Jackson came back to get a picture out of the glove box?"

Elizabeth nodded.

"It was a baby picture. So it must've been Emily's baby girl, the one who passed away. I've heard all about her in our Bible study group. And I've prayed for Emily's heart to be healed..." She paced back and forth and then stopped and looked Elizabeth's way. Her eyes were filled with tears. "It just breaks my heart...for both of them. I could tell Jackson was upset when he got the photo. At the time, I just thought he was sad because of selling his truck, nothing more. If I'd known, I could have said something." She sighed. "I just hope he's okay."

"Me too," Elizabeth said. "I can't speculate about his mental state. I'm only going off of what his neighbor said. But you do know someone who knows him well, Henri, and she might be able to shed some light on all of this."

"So I should call Em? Ask her to get involved?"

"I'm thinking she might already be involved." Elizabeth fought the temptation to tell Henri about the call she'd received from Fred telling her that Emily had turned up at the house on the day after Jackson went missing.

When had all of this gotten so complicated?

CHAPTER FIFTEEN

Mary ended her call with Anna and then turned back to Elizabeth and Henri, who both looked a bit startled. Clearly, she had missed something.

"Well?" Mary shoved her phone into her purse. "What happened? What did I miss?"

Henri brushed her fingers against her forehead to swipe a loose strand of hair out of the way. "Elizabeth just told me that my friend Em is Jackson's wife."

"Ex-wife," Elizabeth corrected.

"Right." Henri nodded. "Ex-wife."

"And you didn't know?" Mary asked.

Henri leaned against the truck, and her gaze shifted to the ground. "I had no clue. I wonder if she even knows that he left home and didn't return. Not that it's any of my business. I'm only just getting to know her, after all. Last night was the first time we've actually spent any time together outside of the group, and we were in a public place, so maybe she didn't feel comfortable telling me there."

"I agree that she probably doesn't know," Mary said. "That's likely, especially if they've been out of touch."

"If they're out of touch, then what was she doing at his house a couple of days ago?" Elizabeth queried. "That's the part I can't figure out. She walked into the house when he was away, like she owned the place. Seems kind of strange to me. She has to know something's up."

"I have no idea." Mary thought about her sister's words. "Maybe we're just overreacting. Maybe Jackson is fine, and we're worrying for nothing."

"I hope so." But Elizabeth's gut was telling her something completely different. She couldn't shake the feeling that Jackson needed help. "I can't put words to it, but somehow I just have this strange sense that he's in some kind of trouble."

"Because the manager of the gas station said he looked ill?" Mary asked. "Is that why you're worried?"

Elizabeth nodded. "Yes. Call it intuition. Call it discernment. I've got the uncanny notion that Jackson Wittmer needs our help."

"So, what do I do?" Henri threw her hands up in the air, as if giving up. "I mean, Em is so sweet. And she's never had anything bad to say about her ex, other than he has problems with alcohol because he never recovered from their little girl's death. She did mention that when we were taking prayer requests at Bible study. But even at that, she didn't seem to hold it against him. She seemed nothing but compassionate. I would almost go so far as to say she still has feelings for him."

Wow. This was news. It floored Elizabeth to think that Henri and Emily were becoming friends. What a small world. Then again, wasn't it just like God to bring people together so the broken could be healed? How good of Him to bring Henri into Emily's life when she really needed a friend.

"Should I call her and ask if she's seen him?" Henri asked. "I don't want to intrude in her personal business, you know? And I sure hope she doesn't think I've just befriended her to get information out of her. That would be awful."

"Right. And this could all be completely innocent," Mary said. "For all we know, Emily might have taken her ex in once they got the news the house was being foreclosed on. Maybe he's over there right now with his feet kicked up, watching Andy Griffith reruns on her television. Stranger things have happened."

"I don't know about that," Henri said. "But maybe she'll open up to me."

"Right. And I'm also inclined to believe Jackson would have told Fred he was staying with his ex," Elizabeth said. "As close as they are, he would have, don't you think?"

"Wait, who's Fred?" Henri asked. "I'm having trouble keeping up with the players."

"He's Jackson's neighbor," Elizabeth explained. "He and Jackson are good friends. I feel sure Jackson would have told Fred if he was staying with Emily."

Mary looked at the anguish on her sister's face and couldn't help but sigh. "You know, Elizabeth, for someone who didn't even know these people a couple of weeks ago, you're sure knotted up over all of this. We don't know if Jackson is truly missing. We have no reason to suspect his ex-wife. I certainly don't know the neighbor well enough to judge him. And…if I'm being totally honest, I don't even know what we're doing standing at a used-car dealership when I really need to be working on wedding decor. To top it all off, we've got a big storm rolling in. Now, if you don't mind, I really think we need to be getting home. I've got work to do."

And at that, she turned and walked back to the car.

Elizabeth listened to Mary fuss all the way home from Lancaster. She didn't really blame her. The trip had taken longer than expected, especially with evening traffic. But they had learned a lot, hadn't they? Henri and Emily were brand-new friends, and they'd met at church, no less. How could you question a friendship that originated at church? And, if everything Henri had said was true, Chester wasn't as bad as the newspaper article implied. Only time would prove her words right or wrong. And even if he turned out to be a slippery salesman, that still didn't implicate him in any way in Jackson's disappearance.

Jackson's disappearance.

Elizabeth chided herself for caring so much. Maybe Mary was right. She was in over her head, caring about someone she barely knew. Perhaps the young man simply wanted to sneak away for a few days, to clear his mind. Maybe he didn't want folks to know where he'd gone because he needed a break from the chaos of his life. Maybe he'd taken the money from the sale of the truck and used it to get away on a much-needed vacation.

On the other hand, why hadn't he used that money to save his home? Wouldn't it make sense to do so, if he had the cash on hand? What had he done with all that money?

Maybe he was too depressed to think clearly. Maybe he'd headed someplace private to put an end to his life. That possibility both terrified her and propelled her to action. But really, what could she do that hadn't already been done? She'd checked out every lead, even gone to the police.

Elizabeth really wanted to swing by Fred Zucker's house one more time but knew that Mary would balk at the idea—in part because of the weather and in part because wedding plans still beckoned. No, her sister had work to do, and Elizabeth wouldn't stand in her way. But Elizabeth would call Fred just as soon as they arrived home, from the privacy of her own room. Her sisters needn't know that her curiosity was still piqued.

Overhead, the skies lurked dark and ominous. A streak of lightning ripped across the patch of gray to the west, and Mary gasped. "Oh, this is awful. I can't believe we might get caught in it."

"I didn't think we'd see rain until tomorrow. And maybe it won't be too bad," Elizabeth said. As if to taunt her, a peal of thunder rumbled in the distance. "Or maybe it will." She kept an eye on the skies, intrigued by the dark color and the sheer magnitude of clouds overhead.

Mary seemed more than a little upset about the weather, if such a thing could be judged from the tight lines around her lips. "If it rains through the weekend, Anna will be so disappointed. And it will affect everything, since a few of the vendors are coming from Lancaster and beyond. Wouldn't it just be awful if some of them had to cancel?"

Elizabeth nodded. Terrible, in fact. To put so many weeks' and months' worth of work into a big day, only to have it rained out? She couldn't even imagine what Anna must be thinking or feeling right now. No doubt she was in a panic.

Just as they pulled off of the highway, Elizabeth's cell phone rang. She groaned when she saw John's name on the screen. "Ugh."

"Who is it?" Mary asked.

"John. Brace yourself. He's not going to be happy that we went over to the car dealership again. Now I'm wishing I hadn't left that message in the first place. Then he wouldn't even know. Oh, why did I have to tell him?"

Mary shook her head. "I'm of the opinion that you needed to tell him. We have to keep the police in the loop, just in case we come across any leads. So you did the right thing."

"I guess you're right." Elizabeth answered the call and did her best to share the news of her visit to Chester's in a laid-back sort of way to make it sound less stressful. She told him about her conversation with Chester and the information she'd received from Henri about Jackson's ex-wife. John chided her for going but seemed relieved that she hadn't gone alone.

"I think it's time for everyone to stay put and focus on the wedding," he said. "From the reports I'm getting, the weather's about to take a turn for the worse, so home is the place to be."

As if to emphasize his point, streaks of lightning ripped across the evening sky, making it look like shattered glass. Elizabeth stared at it, transfixed.

"I have no plans to go out again tonight, I promise," Elizabeth said after a moment of gazing at the sky. And she meant it. She'd stay home and put her feet up. Maybe she'd cuddle up next to the fireplace. It was getting pretty chilly, after all.

"Before you go, I did want to let you know one thing, Elizabeth. An official missing-person report was filed just now."

"Who filed it?"

"Jackson's ex-wife."

"Wow."

"Yes, she just dropped by the station, very worked up. She's convinced he's in bad shape—physically and mentally. And with this bad weather coming in, she was really beside herself. So we went ahead and filed the paperwork."

"I'm so glad."

"Me too. She seems like a nice lady. Said she was going to let his family know."

"So he has family, then. That's good."

"Yes." John cleared his throat. "She plans to contact them right away."

Another peal of thunder caused the car to shake, and Elizabeth startled. "Whoa."

"Yeah. I'd better let you go. Just wanted you to know."

"Thanks for calling, John."

She ended the call and turned back to Mary just as they turned onto Ronks Road. "How much of that did you figure out?"

"Jackson's wife filed a missing-person report?"

"Yes." Elizabeth nodded.

"Do you think Henri called her after we left the car dealership?"

"Maybe." Elizabeth shrugged. "If so, she must have been concerned too."

"No kidding." May paused. "But the fact that his ex-wife filed the report tells me a lot about her. She must still care about him."

"True. Oh, and get this—John said Jackson has family as well, so I feel better knowing the ex-wife has contacted them."

"Yes, that's a relief."

"I didn't mention that we gave Henri our business card. He was upset that I left one at the gas station."

Mary slowed the car as they approached their driveway. "She needs to know how to contact us in case she learns anything new about Emily and Jackson. Besides, people know where we live. We don't exactly hide that information. Everyone can see that we're a family-run business and that we live right by the shop."

"True. I'd never considered the fact that that might make us more vulnerable, though."

"Vulnerable to what?"

"I don't know," Elizabeth said. "Just...vulnerable. Most business owners lock their stores up at night and drive home to unknown locations. We're right here, in plain view." She gestured to the farm, which looked a bit eerie under the flashing night sky.

"Don't go getting paranoid on me." Mary gripped the steering wheel as lightning flashed again. "It's creepy enough out here tonight."

"True," Elizabeth agreed.

As Mary pulled up the driveway, Elizabeth couldn't help but breathe a sigh of relief. She just wanted to go inside, find something to eat, and spend a quiet evening resting.

As soon as Mary slipped the car into PARK, Elizabeth got out and walked toward the house. She turned back to her sister with what she hoped would look like a convincing smile. "Thanks for going with me, Mary. I feel better after talking to Henri."

"Me too. I'm glad she's in the loop. And I'm sorry I was so cranky back there. I'm just nervous about the wedding. We're getting close, and I'm wondering if it'll all come together. I'm starting to wonder if Martha and I have taken on too much. I accused you of getting too involved with this investigation when I'm the one who's up to my eyeballs in someone else's event."

"I'm sure both stories will work out fine—the wedding and Jackson's story, whatever it is. And I don't think you're overcommitted, Mary. You're so good at what you do."

"Thank you, Lizzie. That means a lot."

"You're welcome. You and Martha are both amazing. I'd be willing to bet she's in the kitchen right now, humming along as she whips up layer after layer of delectable wedding cake. And you're going to get those signs done. It'll all work out, I'm sure. These things always do."

"I hope you're right," Mary said. "Thanks for the encouragement, regardless."

"You're welcome." Another crack of thunder was followed by the brightest, most electrifying streak of lightning Elizabeth had ever seen. It took her breath away as she stared up at the sky. "Now let's get inside before this storm lands right on top of us."

"Looks like it already has. I wonder how Martha's holding up."

They walked into the farmhouse and found their sister hard at work in the kitchen. Her apron was covered in flour, and she had cake batter smeared across her cheek. Her hair, which she'd pulled up into a twist, had telltale signs of flour in it as well. She was mumbling something Elizabeth couldn't quite make out as she dumped flour into the large stand mixer.

As they drew near, Martha put up her hands in exaggerated despair, and her lips curled down in a deep frown. "Sure, *now* you come back, when I'm almost done. Why would you leave me in my hour of desperation?"

CHAPTER SIXTEEN

Hour of desperation?"

Elizabeth stared at the kitchen in disbelief. The sink was filled with dirty dishes. The countertops were loaded with baking pans of every conceivable size. And the dogs were having a wonderful time lapping up what was either flour or powdered sugar all over the floor.

Mary dropped her purse onto one of the kitchen chairs and went straight to the sink to start loading dirty dishes into the dishwasher. "Um, you're the one who told us we should go, remember? You were excited about having the kitchen to yourself, as I recall."

Martha shook her head. "That was before I dropped a carton of cream on the floor and then slid halfway across the room like a skier headed down a cliff."

"Oh my goodness. Are you all right?" Elizabeth set her purse on the counter.

"Don't put that there!" Martha gestured to the purse. "I need every available inch of counter space right now. Please put that in the other room."

"Okay, okay." Elizabeth carried her purse into the other room and then returned empty-handed. "Now, answer my question. Are. You. All. Right?"

"I'm fine," Martha said. She mumbled something else under her breath and then counted the eggs in the open carton. She got to the number seven and groaned. Loudly.

"Sure you are." Mary turned away from her work at the dishwasher and stared their sister down. "I don't know if you realize this, Martha, but you have batter in your hair."

"Oh." She swiped at it and groaned again. "Who cares? At the moment, I've got bigger problems. I can't remember how many eggs whites I've already added to this cake batter. I'm working on a double recipe, so I need eight total, and I think I've only put in seven, but I'm not sure."

"Count the shells," Mary suggested as she shoved a few more bowls into the already crowded dishwasher and closed the door. "If anyone needs me, I'll be working on the signs for the wedding." She turned on the dishwasher and walked out of the room.

"I would count the shells," Martha called out as Mary left the room, "but this is my third batch, and I've got all the shells from the previous batches in the trash can." She sighed. "Oh well. I'm going to assume I've only added seven. I'll put in one more. It shouldn't hurt it."

Elizabeth watched in amazement as her sister got more and more frazzled when she added another egg and turned on the mixer. Martha did tend to get worked up from time to time, but this was a bit extreme, even for her. "I'll have to trust your judgment on that one, Martha," she said. "I'm not much of a baker. I'm sorry you're under the gun though. Seems like a big project."

"Yes, and I wouldn't mind waiting until tomorrow, but I'm trying to get the baking done before the storm blows through. You know how barometric pressure affects cake."

Elizabeth had no idea, but wouldn't bother admitting it.

Martha went on and on about a cake she'd once baked that had collapsed, her voice rising to be heard above the mixer, but Elizabeth was distracted by the buzzing of her phone. She answered it and was surprised to hear Henri's voice on the other end of the line. The young woman sounded rushed and a little frazzled.

"Elizabeth, is that you?"

"It is," she responded.

"I wanted you to know that I called Em after you left the car lot."

"Oh?" She shifted the phone to the other ear and sat down at the table. "What did you learn?"

"Well…" Henri's voice grew more animated. "She was surprised to hear that I had met Jackson and even more shocked to hear that we've been looking for him. She told me she was going straight to the police department to file a missing-person report."

"She did that. I just got word."

"Good. She also told me that she stopped by his place a couple of days ago to pick up some things. She told me that she'd called first and left a message, but he never responded, so she took a chance and went anyway. He wasn't there when she arrived, but the house was unlocked, so she went inside to get the things she needed. I guess the house is being foreclosed on?

Something like that? She'd gotten a call from the mortgage company, she said."

"I guess that explains why she was there."

"Right. Anyway, she wanted to get some of the baby's things she'd left behind when she moved out. She told me that she left Jackson a note to call her, but he never did."

"Wow. So she really didn't know he hadn't been at the house since Saturday at that point?"

"No. She just figured he'd gone out to the store or something. She saw that the truck wasn't in the driveway but didn't even realize he'd sold it until I told her. Apparently that truck really meant a lot to him."

"I'm surprised Fred didn't mention it to her."

"Fred. That's the elderly neighbor, right?"

"Right."

"I don't think she talked to him. She said she saw him out in his yard, but he didn't mention that Jackson was missing or anything like that."

"Right. He was probably trying to stay out of it. So how did she take the news?"

"She's worried sick. I still think she still has feelings for him. She contacted me about thirty minutes later to tell me she'd reached out to the police and to extended family, just to make sure he hadn't turned up."

"And he hadn't?"

"From what I understand, they weren't home, so she left a message. But she said they're really good people, and they'll let her know if they hear from him."

"Ah, good. Well, hopefully he's with them, safe and sound."

"Yes, I sure hope so. She's not pinning much hope on it, though, because he's been estranged from them for years. Anyway, I feel awful, thinking something might've happened to him. And can you even imagine being out in this storm? It's scary out there!"

"No. I wouldn't wish this on my worst enemy."

"Me neither. Well, anyway, I'll be praying. Thanks again for sharing the news with me. And just for the record, I really think this news story about Chester is overblown. Time will prove me right...or wrong. In the meantime, maybe you could be praying about that too. God has a way of bringing the truth to light—in His own time and His own way."

"Absolutely. I'll be praying. Thanks for calling, Henri."

Elizabeth ended the call and turned to her sister. Before she could say a word, a crash of thunder pealed, and the room shook.

"Great, just great." Martha muttered something under her breath and turned up the speed on the mixer. It drowned out whatever she was saying.

Elizabeth decided to slip out of the room for a few minutes to make a call to Fred Zucker. Alone in her room, she pulled out her cell phone and punched in his number. While she was waiting for him to answer, she walked over to the window and pulled back the curtain. The skies sure looked dark. Well, except for the crazy zigzags of lightning, which streaked from one side to the other.

Fred answered with an abrupt, "This had better be important. You're making me miss *Matlock*."

Okay then.

"Fred, sorry to interrupt. This is Elizabeth Classen calling again."

"Blue blouse or pink blouse?"

"Blue." She paused. "I'm really sorry to interrupt. I can call back later, once your show ends. I just wanted to ask a few questions."

"Nah, that's okay. I can pause this TV. Give me a minute so I can find the remote." He disappeared for a good two or three minutes, then returned to the call sounding more frazzled than before. "Well, Blue Blouse, if you're calling to ask about Rocky, I can tell you things aren't going so well. I don't know if it's this storm or something else, but he won't stop wailing. It's about to drive me out of my ever-lovin' mind, if you want the truth of it. That's why I had the TV turned up so loud, to drown him out. It's not working though. And to top things off, I can't seem to find my glasses. I can't figure out the remote without them. Just part of getting old, I guess. Jackson was always so helpful when I had trouble with the remote." He sighed.

"I'm sorry. Do you think Rocky's missing Jackson?"

Fred heaved a loud sigh. "Yeah, I'm sure that's it. And, truth be told, I'm missing him too. I usually see him at least once or twice a day. We talk—about the weather, our lives, everything. So it's just plain weird not to have him around. And a little unnerving, if you want the truth, especially in a storm like this. I'd feel better if I knew where he was."

"Me too."

"Did that cop-fella tell you that I talked to the gas station manager? He saw Jackson a couple days back."

"He did. That was quite a relief."

"Yep. But it's been two days since then, and I still haven't heard from him. It's just not like Jackson to do this, you know? And if it's true that he's sick, then he needs a doctor."

"Agreed." An idea hit her at once. "Fred, that's it! Tomorrow morning I'll make some calls to local clinics or hospitals to find out if he's been to any of them."

"What about confidentiality laws?" Fred countered. "Would they even tell you if he was a patient?"

Her enthusiasm deflated. "Oh, good point. I don't know." Elizabeth paused to think it through. Maybe John would make the calls for her.

"I can't help wondering what happened to the money Chester paid him for that truck," Fred said. "I just hope he wasn't carrying around cash."

"Surely he was paid with a cashier's check," Elizabeth said.

"Hope so. I know he was hoping to use that money to save the house, but now I don't know what to think." He paused. "I'd feel better if he'd just come home. Not that he has a home to come back to. His house is all locked up now."

"Right," she agreed. "I'm just afraid that some people get really down in the dumps and slip away..."

"To hurt themselves?"

"Yes. I didn't want to say it out loud, but yes. Do you think he could have been that depressed?"

"Maybe." Fred's words were laced with concern. "I should've gone with him on Saturday. Should've offered to drive him to the store. I've been beating myself up over it all week long. But how could I have known he wasn't planning to come back?"

"You couldn't."

"And as for your question about doing himself in, I guess some folks'd say that the alcohol he drinks is a slow, steady road to the inevitable, but Jackson probably doesn't see it that way."

"I'm sure he doesn't."

As another streak of lightning lit the window, the lights flickered. From downstairs she heard Martha cry out, "No!"

"That was a doozy! Everything okay over there?" Fred asked.

"Yes, but our lights keep going on and off."

"Same here. And Rocky's not liking it, one little bit."

"Me neither. My sister's trying to bake a wedding cake. That's hard to do without power."

"Pink Blouse is a baker?"

"No, my other sister, Martha." Elizabeth paused. "Anyway, Fred, I've been wondering about something else. Jackson sold the truck on Saturday, so he had money on him when you saw him last."

"Yep, and don't think I haven't thought about that. I know he planned to use it to try to save the house, but when the foreclosure sign went up on Wednesday morning I knew for sure he hadn't made it to the bank in time. That scared me more than anything, I think. And the fact that he might be out there with a large sum of money doesn't make me feel much better about his situation. I just hope he doesn't squander it on, well, you know."

"Right. One more thing—it's about Emily."

"What about her?"

"You said you saw her come to the house on Tuesday, right?"

"Yes, that's right."

"Did you mention that Jackson was missing?"

"No. I watched her from the side yard but never said a word." Fred paused. When he finally spoke, his words were slow. "Don't you see? I didn't want to go sticking my nose into her business. I'm close to Jackson, and he confides in me, but Emily…that's another story altogether. And remember what I said before—I wasn't sure but what he might be with another lady friend, if you catch my drift. Though I really couldn't picture it, since he's really not over Emily. But I've seen men go a little crazy when they're heartbroken, especially if they've got a little alcohol in them."

"I understand. I was just checking."

The lights flickered once again, and Martha let out another cry from the kitchen below.

Elizabeth flinched as a peal of thunder shook her room. "I guess I'd better let you go, Fred. Thanks for answering my questions."

"Stay safe over there, Blue Blouse," Fred responded. "I have a feeling things are gonna get worse before they get better."

Martha scurried around the kitchen in a frenzy. The sooner she got this final round of cakes into the oven, the sooner they'd be baked. And the sooner they got baked, the greater her chances of not ruining this wedding.

"Please, Lord!" she said aloud. "Please let the power stay on long enough to get this done."

She already had the barometric pressure against her. If the power went out…no, she wouldn't think about that, not with so much to be done.

Mary entered the kitchen, eyes wide. "I finished the signs. What can I do to help speed up this process so you can get some sleep tonight?"

"Grease and flour those three cake pans." Martha pointed to the three twelve-inch pans sitting on the counter. "I've got to get them in the oven, or this wedding cake will only have three tiers instead of four."

"Would that be so awful?"

Martha looked Mary's way, stunned. "Are you serious? If I skip the twelve-inch tier, close to sixty people won't get cake."

"Oh." Mary looked pretty clueless.

Martha felt as if her heart might explode in her chest as another peal of thunder rumbled. Her hands trembled as she reached for the shortening to help her sister grease the pans. "Please, Lord," she whispered, "just one more round before we lose power."

The lights flickered again, and she tried to steady her breathing as she filled the pans that Mary prepared. She pulled the ten-inch cakes out of the oven, but there was only room for two of the three twelve-inchers. Great. She would just have to pray for the best.

"It's just a cake, Martha." The words came from Elizabeth, who entered the kitchen and walked to the table.

"To you, it's just a cake. To me, it's hours and hours of work gone down the tubes if we lose power. I've got to get this done so the cakes can chill overnight. Tomorrow I'll fill and stack them."

Elizabeth gave her a blank stare. Either she didn't understand or didn't see the urgency in all of this.

"You can always bake tomorrow, is all I'm saying."

"I'm supposed to help Mary and Anna decorate the barn for the wedding, remember?" Martha bit back the sigh that threatened to escape. "Besides, I don't want to have to start over. So please pray. That's all I'm asking."

She'd barely gotten the words out when a crack of thunder shook the room…and the house went dark.

CHAPTER SEVENTEEN

"Everyone okay?" Mary's voice rang out from across the dark kitchen.

"I'm okay," Elizabeth responded. She couldn't stop shaking though. Maybe it had something to do with the sudden darkness, or perhaps it had more to do with Martha's cries of anguish over the cakes in the oven. Her sister wasn't taking the news of this blackout well at all. Not that Elizabeth blamed her. It would be awful to put this much work into something only to have it fail in the end due to circumstances beyond your control.

Elizabeth reached for her phone and turned on the flashlight app. She pointed it at the stove, relief sweeping over her. "Martha, it's a gas oven. Remember?"

"Yes, but the igniter is electric." These words came from Mary. "I'm not sure if it will keep the right temp now."

"Ah." Elizabeth nodded, though obviously no one could see her. "What can we do?"

"I say we leave the cakes in as long as we can," Mary suggested.

"Yes, maybe the residual heat will keep them baking for a few minutes. I don't know." Martha plopped down into a kitchen chair and put her head on the table.

"Can I help you get the cooled cakes into the fridge?" Elizabeth asked. "We could wrap and stack them."

"The fridge is electric too." Martha's words were laced with emotion and fear. "Don't you see? It's ruined. Everything is ruined."

"Don't be silly." Mary's voice took on a motherly tone. "You've got three full tiers of cake baked. If the power doesn't come back on you can make new batter for the bottom tier in the morning. Don't panic, Martha. You got started on this project plenty early, and it will end well. I feel sure of it."

"I'm doing my best."

Elizabeth set her phone down on the table with the beam from the flashlight pointing up. She would gather the cooked cakes and get them refrigerated. Even if they lost power, the cakes would be just fine in the fridge overnight.

She had just wrapped the second tier cakes when she was startled by the sound of the wind knocking tree limbs into the side of the house.

"Did...did you hear that?" Martha asked. "Sounds like the trees are about to rip through the side of the house."

The wind began to howl, a slow, painful howl, and the dogs decided to join in. Tink started her high-pitched yapping, and Pal added his voice to the fray, his barks short and frantic. On and on they went, growing more animated with each passing second.

"Calm down, you two!" Mary called out. "That's the last thing we need."

Thankfully, the dogs quieted down. Still, Elizabeth could hear the low growl at the back of Tink's throat.

A light flashed across the kitchen window. It seemed different from the streaks of lightning, as if coming from someplace lower. Elizabeth tried not to think too much about it, but something was definitely amiss outside. She could feel it. From outside the house, she heard what sounded like the whinnying of horses. Strange. Tink started growling in earnest now.

"Did you hear that?" Martha asked. "It sounded like—"

A peal of thunder shook the room again. Lightning flashed immediately afterward. Tink's growl became full-out barking once again, which only served to put a shiver down Elizabeth's spine. Could this night possibly get any creepier?

"The storm must be right on top of us." Mary's words came from out of the darkness. "They say you can always tell when thunder and lightning come together. I'm sure that's why the dogs are spooked."

"Yes, but I thought I heard something else," Martha said. "It sounded like—"

"Horses." Elizabeth finished for her.

"Yes. Who would be out with horses in this mess?"

"I would hate to be out in it, that's for sure." Elizabeth felt a sudden chill and pulled her sweater tighter. "I'm so glad we made it home from Lancaster before this hit. And to think, all I wanted to do tonight was take a hot bath and relax."

"Relax?" Martha's voice took on a shrill tone. "Who has time to relax?"

The dogs calmed down, and the storm seemed to quiet itself as well. The lights flickered, as if to give them hope, then the world went dark once again.

"Terrific," Martha muttered. "These cakes are going to be ruined."

"Deep breath, Martha," Mary said, her voice steady and strong. "This is a life test, and you're going to pass it with flying colors."

"I'm not so sure about that," Martha responded. "And I can think of a thousand other tests I'd rather take right now. Have I mentioned the fact that barometric pressure affects a cake's ability to rise?"

"About a dozen times," Mary said. "But who's counting?"

"The cakes are almost done now, Martha," Elizabeth said. "Don't fret."

"Me? Fret?"

Mary laughed. "If you want my opinion, I think it's funny that we're sitting here in Amish country fretting over losing our power. We're so accustomed to modern living that we don't know how to live without it. Our Amish neighbors aren't panicking tonight. Only us Englischers."

"I'm not so sure about that. Listen! Is that hail?" Martha's voice grew more animated. "For pity's sake, it is! It's hailing out there!"

"Sure sounds like it," Mary said. "Either that, or God's dropping marbles on the house."

Mary's cell phone rang, and Elizabeth went back to wrapping cakes as Mary answered it. "Yes, Anna, we're fine." Mary paused. "I'm right here in the kitchen with Martha and Elizabeth. The cakes are mostly baked, so stop fretting." Another pause followed. "You have nothing to worry about, honey. I'm sure this will pass in a hurry. You'll see." Another pause. "Yes, I know the ground will be wet, but the ceremony is inside the barn, remember? It'll be okay, Anna. Take a deep breath." A lengthy pause. "Yes, I'll still be there in the morning to help you decorate the barn, regardless. I promise. I won't let you down." She carried on with the conversation for a couple more minutes and ended the call.

"Oh boy," Elizabeth said. "I'm guessing she's a wreck."

"That's putting it mildly." Mary cleared her throat. "But I think I calmed her down. I hope so, anyway. At this point I'm just glad the wedding isn't until Saturday morning. Tomorrow's going to be pretty nasty, but we'll get through it."

Another flash of lightning streaked across the sky, visible from the kitchen window. Thunder followed, and the dogs started barking again. This time they wouldn't be stilled. Tink ran toward the front door, barking hysterically.

"What in the world?" Elizabeth strained to hear through the yapping. "Is that someone knocking?"

Sure enough. Someone was definitely at the front door.

"Are we expecting anyone?" Martha called out above the din.

"Not that I know of," Elizabeth said. "You don't suppose it's Anna, do you?"

"Surely not," Mary said. "I just got off the phone with her. I made her promise she'd settle in after her dinner with the family, and she agreed to that."

Another knock sounded.

Elizabeth reached for her phone. "I'll get it. Keep wrapping those cake layers, Mary. And make more room in the fridge, just in case those final layers do bake through."

Elizabeth made her way through the living room to the front door, using the tiny beam of light from her phone to light the way. She called out, "Who's there?" just to be safe, but couldn't quite make out the voice on the other side.

She cracked the door and saw shadowy images of someone—or a couple of someones—on the porch.

"Elizabeth! Oh, Elizabeth! We've had an accident! Our buggy went into the ditch in front of your house!"

She pulled the door open and angled the flashlight just so. In that moment she saw Susanna Wittmer standing there with her brother Frankie.

"For pity's sake! Come in out of this weather!" She beamed the light into the doorway to guide them, and seconds later Susanna and Frankie were inside.

"Thank you so much!" Susanna's voice trembled. "I...I..."

"Thank you for taking us in," Frankie said. "We did not know what else to do."

"What on earth has happened?" Elizabeth asked.

"We were making our way down Ronks Road, and everything went dark," Frankie explained. "I think one of the horses got spooked. He reared up and nearly toppled us."

"Oh my goodness." Elizabeth clutched a hand to her chest. "That's awful!"

"Scared me to death, Elizabeth!" Susanna's voice trembled. "I have never prayed that hard in my life."

"I tried to get the horse under control," Frankie explained. "But the next thing you know we were headed right for the ditch."

The very idea terrified Elizabeth. To think, all of this had happened just outside her own home while she was safely tucked inside. "I'm so glad you're both all right." She paused. "You *are* all right, aren't you?"

"Yes," Susanna and Frankie spoke in unison.

"Just shaken up a bit," Susanna explained. "And I am sure I will have a few bruises on my cheek from where I landed against the edge of the buggy. But nothing is broken, that I can tell."

"Good. Are the horses okay?"

"Yes. I got them out of the ditch and hitched them to the fence post," Frankie said. "But the buggy is lodged in mud."

"The water in that ditch is deep," Susanna said. "Probably a foot or more. I will need to call for help once this storm calms down a bit."

"Please, come into the kitchen and warm up. I'll see if I can track down some towels." Elizabeth led the way into the kitchen, where her sisters greeted their guests with great concern. Martha went to retrieve some bath towels and gave them to Susanna and Frankie. Outside, the storm continued to rage. In fact, the peals of thunder served as a notice that this monster planned to rage a while longer still.

"Please, take a seat, you two," Martha said.

Elizabeth beamed the tiny light from her phone toward the breakfast table. Susanna and Frankie sat, towels in hand.

"I hate to get your chairs w-w-wet." Susanna shivered.

"Don't be silly," Elizabeth chided her. "The furniture's the very last thing on my mind right now, trust me. You two just sit and rest. I think we've still got some coffee in the coffeepot. It was hot before the power went out, so I'm sure it's still plenty warm. Could I interest you in a cup?"

Susanna and Frankie both nodded.

Elizabeth poured out two cups, and before long they were all seated at the table.

After a few sips, Susanna seemed to calm down a bit. "I cannot quite make out the kitchen in the dark, but I have a notion we have walked in on something."

"Yes, it smells mighty good in here," Frankie said.

"Wedding cake," Martha explained. "Our childhood friend Anna is getting married. Do you remember her?"

"A little, maybe? Englischer?" Susanna asked.

"Yes," Martha said. "I was right in the middle of baking when the power went out. I've got cakes in the oven right now, but I'm sure they're ruined." Just as she said the last words, the power came back on.

Martha's face was awash with relief as she peeked through the oven door's window at her cakes.

Elizabeth turned back to Susanna. "When this lets up we can give you all a ride home."

Frankie shook his head. "There is no need to get you out tonight. If you will let me use your phone to make a call, I will get help to pull the buggy out of the ditch."

"Of course." Elizabeth pressed her cell phone into his hand.

Minutes later, Susanna and Frankie's older brother George arrived, just as the winds and rain ceased. He and Frankie headed out to deal with the buggy. Susanna remained behind. She offered to help in the kitchen, and as they worked on dishes, Elizabeth glanced her friend's way and smiled.

"I'm puzzled by one thing, Susanna. I thought you were gone until tomorrow morning. Why did you come home early?"

"Ah." Susanna looked up from the cake pan she was drying. "We heard a storm was coming in, so our hired car brought us back from Philadelphia a few hours ago. I should not have asked Frankie to take me back out in this weather, but I was trying to make it to my sister-in-law's place. We have just had some terrible news, Elizabeth."

"Terrible news? Oh no!" She set her dishcloth down and stared at her friend. "What's happened?"

"Yes, it is such a shock." Susanna's voice broke. "You see, we have just heard that our baby brother has gone missing."

CHAPTER EIGHTEEN

"Wait." Elizabeth couldn't believe her ears. "Susanna, is your brother's name Jackson?"

"Yes."

Elizabeth very nearly dropped the towel in her hand. Mary stood on the far side of the room, jaw dropped. Martha was too focused on the cakes to pay the conversation much mind, but for a moment, the room grew completely silent. Elizabeth could scarcely believe what she was hearing.

Susanna's concern seemed to lift for a moment. "I was not sure if you would remember him though, Elizabeth. He has been gone for years. The big mess between Daed and Jackson happened while you were away."

"I don't remember him."

"Did he go by another name back then or something?" Mary asked.

"Who?" Martha seemed to snap to attention. "Who are we talking about? What did I miss?"

"Jackson Wittmer," Elizabeth explained. "He's Susanna's younger brother."

"Wait...the man you've been searching for is Susanna's brother?" Martha set one of the cakes on a cooling rack and gave them a pensive look. "Why didn't you tell me that before?"

"Because I'm just now finding out," Elizabeth explained. "I knew in my gut there must be some sort of link. The Wittmer name was too much of a coincidence. Maybe that's why the Lord has had me searching so hard for him."

"You have been searching for Jakey?" Susanna looked astounded by this news. "Really? We did not even know he was missing until we returned this afternoon. We have been out of touch for years."

"We've been on the hunt for several days, actually. It's kind of a long story, Susanna. And is that what you call him...Jakey?"

"Yes. He never went by Jackson as a boy," Susanna said. "Everyone around these parts knew him as Little Jake or Jakey."

"Oh my goodness." Martha's face lit with recognition. "Little Jakey. I *do* remember him." She lifted the cake pan, flipped it upside down, and turned out the cake onto the cooling rack.

"Didn't he move away when he was just sixteen or seventeen, something like that?" Mary asked.

Susanna nodded. "Yes, he spent his *rumspringa* doing wild things—crazy things. Drinking, partying, driving fast cars. I guess he really enjoyed life outside the confines of the walls he grew up in. When rumspringa ended, he made the decision not to return to the church or to be baptized. It was hard for Daed and Maam. Very hard. To their way of thinking, Jakey had turned his back on everything they held dear. Their hopes and dreams for him seemed lost. We were all brokenhearted."

"No doubt." Elizabeth felt so sorry for the family, losing their son in such a way. But they finally had the answer to the one question that had lingered for days. Jackson Wittmer was definitely part of the larger Wittmer family. So much for

Fred Zucker's comment that Jackson hadn't been raised in the Amish community. Boy, would he be surprised to hear all of this. Still, Jackson had deliberately chosen a life as an Englischer over his Amish upbringing. Most Amish teens returned to their roots, even after rumspringa. They enjoyed their season of wild living but returned to the fold to live quiet, unencumbered lives.

"We'd heard that Jakey joined the Marines," Susanna said. "One of the local boys told us. Daed took the news hard."

"Ah." Elizabeth knew the Amish were pacifists and had strong views against military service. Jackson's decision to serve in the Marines surely took him far away from the life he'd once known.

"We heard he was serving overseas. Then years went by, and we lost touch." Susanna clasped her hands. "Daed did not even want to hear his name mentioned."

"Did you realize he'd married and moved to Lancaster?" Elizabeth asked.

"Yes, his wife reached out to us right after they married, but our relationship was so strained at that point, and you know how strict my daed was. He did not want any part of their new life."

Mary looked up from her work. "That's just so sad," she said.

"Yes, especially over the past few days," Susanna responded. "We tried to contact Emily to let her know that Daed had passed away, but her number had changed. We had no address, no way of contacting him."

"So Jackson doesn't know." Elizabeth could only imagine how devastated he would be to receive the news after the fact.

"Unless someone passed on word," Susanna said. "But if any of our friends have stayed in touch with him, they have not told us. I have felt so disconnected. Would you believe I just found out today that Emily and Jackson are divorced? Such sad business."

"Did she tell you that they lost their baby?" Elizabeth asked.

"Yes." Susanna looked shocked by Elizabeth's proclamation. "But how did you know that?"

"Susanna…I think maybe you'd better sit down for a few minutes. I have some things to tell you, but it's going to take a while."

Susanna took a seat at the table, and Martha offered her a fresh cup of coffee. Elizabeth then went through the details of what had happened, starting with Jackson showing up at the shop with the pitcher.

"Oh, Elizabeth!" Susanna's eyes misted over, and she clasped her hands together. "Emily mentioned the pitcher in her call! She said she has been frantic over it. Absolutely frantic."

"She has?"

"Yes. She told me that she went back to their house on Tuesday. She knew it was about to be foreclosed on and wanted to get the pitcher out before the bank took over. She had every intention of returning it to us. But when she got there, the pitcher was missing."

"Because Jackson had already sold it to us."

Martha took a seat across from them and fanned herself with a potholder. "One thing I don't understand—if Jackson knew it was so important to the family, why wouldn't he just bring it back to you in the first place?"

"Shame? Embarrassment? I do not know. I cannot begin to guess why he would have sold it, other than desperation to hold on to the house. It is such a valuable piece, and not just in the way you think."

"Far more valuable than we knew when I purchased it from him," Elizabeth explained. "I only gave him a fraction of what it was worth. I had absolutely no idea of its value."

"It means far more to us than dollars and cents, Elizabeth," Susanna said. "When Jackson told Maam that he was leaving the farm, she insisted that he take the pitcher with him."

"Why the pitcher?"

"She said it represented an empty life, which is what she was afraid he would live outside of the family. She wanted him to look at it and see that there was a better way to leading a full life than the road he was taking."

"Your maam was a very wise woman," Mary said.

"Yes. And she wanted him to know how much he would be missed. Maam said that a piece of her heart would be missing as long as he was gone. So she deliberately gave up one of her most treasured items as a reminder that nothing would be the same until he returned."

"Oh my." The story hit Elizabeth hard and left a lump in her throat.

Susanna continued. "She made him promise he would bring it back someday. I think she always felt he would return and the pitcher was like…I don't know…an insurance policy?"

"Oh my goodness." Martha looked away from the oven long enough to gasp at this news.

"That's heartbreaking," Mary added.

"Yes." Susanna frowned. "Even sadder, she passed away a few years later, and Jackson was not there for her service. By then, he and Em had lost the baby. Daed took it really hard. The rest of us did too."

Elizabeth sighed. "No doubt."

"Em told us that she has started going back to church again." Susanna's somber expression shifted to delight. "I think she has made some new friends too. So maybe she will stay put. I truly believe God can heal her broken heart, and it brings me such joy to know He is bringing people into her life to help with that process."

"I might know a little something about that too." Elizabeth felt a rush of joy as she thought about Henri's new friendship with Emily. "But I guess I can fill you in later. I think we can safely say that God is on the move. He's got all the players in place for wonderful things to happen."

"Always," Susanna agreed. "Which is why I have to believe we will see this situation with Jackson turn around too. We just have to. Too many years have passed already. I do not want another day to go by without seeing my brother."

"I pray you'll see him one day soon," Elizabeth said. "But I can guarantee you'll see the pitcher. Excuse me just a minute, Susanna. There's something I need to take care of."

"Of course."

"I'll be right back, I promise." With her heart in her throat, Elizabeth used her phone for a flashlight and trucked across the muddy drive to the shop, where she made her way inside to retrieve the porcelain pitcher from the stockroom. She held it carefully as she traversed the path back to the farmhouse across the soggy ground. More than anything, she wanted to get this precious pitcher into her friend's waiting arms.

When she entered the kitchen, she found Susanna eating wedding cake scraps—the bits Martha had shaved off the tops of the cake layers.

"I could not help myself." Susanna giggled. She looked up from her plate and gasped as she saw the pitcher. "Oh, Elizabeth!" Tears rolled over her lashes as she reached to touch it. "Maam would be so happy to see it." She picked up the pitcher and hugged it to her chest. "But she would be heartbroken to know that Jackson was not home too. It was meant to be a… what do you call it? A package deal."

"I haven't given up on finding him, Susanna." Elizabeth picked up the story where she'd left off, starting with the morning Rocky had shown up at Secondhand Blessings without his owner. When she got to the point where she'd seen the Wittmer name on the mailbox outside of Jackson's house, Susanna flinched.

"I do not understand why you did not tell me you were looking for someone with the same name. I would have explained our story," she said.

"I tried, Susanna. And I didn't know he was related, honestly. There are a lot of Wittmers in Lancaster County, you know? By the time I found out you were out of town, I was up to my eyeballs in trying to track him down. I've been genuinely worried about Jackson. We all have."

Susanna's lashes brimmed with fresh tears. "As are we. Em said she did not really think much of it when she found the house empty on Tuesday. She said Jackson was often with the neighbor."

"Mr. Zucker. He's taking care of Rocky right now. We saw both of them the other night. From what we could gather, Fred has become a father figure of sorts to Jackson."

"I am so glad to hear this. He has needed one so badly." Susanna's eyes filled with tears again. "And now he is gone, and no one knows where. I would not even know where to start looking. That is how disconnected I am from my own brother." She began to cry in earnest now.

Elizabeth rested her hand on Susanna's back. "It's okay, Susanna. He's the one who made the choice to leave, not you."

"I know, but too many years have gone by. I could not begin to tell you what is going through his head or where he might have gone off to. I had no idea until today that he struggled with depression or had a problem with alcohol."

"Yes, we heard that too." Mary sat next to Susanna and took her hand.

"This is all so hard to take in." Susanna shook her head. "Emily said the last time she saw Jakey he looked really bad, much older than his years. It really startled her."

"Yes, I was surprised to hear he was only in his early thirties," Elizabeth admitted. "Kind of shocked me, actually."

A knock sounded at the door, and a voice rang out. "Okay to come in?"

"Of course, Frankie," Mary called out. "Come on in and get some hot coffee."

Frankie and his brother George joined them, and Susanna brought them up to speed on what she'd learned. They were stunned to see the pitcher and thrilled to take it home with them.

"Now you see why I could not sell the matching washbasin," Susanna explained.

"Of course!" Elizabeth said. "I only wish I'd known then what I know now. Then I could have given the pitcher to you right away."

Susanna rose, still clutching the pitcher to her chest. "Are you sure you want me to take it, Elizabeth? You paid for it, fair and square."

"Hardly fair and square. As I said, I had no idea it was so valuable. Please take it. It will ease my conscience and will bring joy to your family too. That means the world to me."

Her sisters chimed in in agreement.

"It's yours," Mary insisted. "The lost sheep returning to the fold."

"The lost sheep returning to the fold." Susanna repeated the words, her eyes filling with tears. "Now we must pray that Jackson will do the same. Oh, please pray, ladies. I do not want to give in to fear, but right now it is wrapping around my heart so tight I can barely breathe. We want our brother back. No matter where he has been, no matter what he has done, he is family, and we need him in our lives."

"Yes, amen," Frankie echoed.

Susanna's plea broke Elizabeth's heart. She promised to pray and followed her friends to the front door to say goodbye as they left.

"Well, that was certainly heartbreaking," Mary said.

"Did you have a hunch all along that Jackson was related to Susanna?" Martha asked.

"With so many Wittmers in the area? And nothing about him said, 'I used to be Amish.' You know? Just the opposite, in fact."

"Right." Mary nodded. "I agree with that."

"For that matter, Fred Zucker has a familiar last name too, but I'm convinced he was never Amish. Many of these surnames are linked to the Amish a few generations back, I suppose." She paused and thought about Susanna's story of her brother leaving after rumspringa. If anything, it propelled Elizabeth to try harder to locate Jackson, no matter how long it took.

A short while later, just before settling into bed, Elizabeth found herself pacing the room and praying for Jackson in earnest. "Wherever he is, Lord, please watch over him. Bring him home. Return him to those who love him. Remind him that he is loved and that You have great plans for his life. Don't let him forget that he is valuable, not just to You, but to his family and to Fred too. Guard his heart, I pray."

She felt a particular urgency to pray for Jackson's protection, so she spent some time doing that as well. Then she flipped off the light and climbed into bed.

Elizabeth pulled the quilt up to her chin, shivering against a sudden chill that had overtaken her. Her eyes fluttered closed, and she was finally free to rest.

Overhead a crack of thunder shook the house. Elizabeth could hardly believe her ears as the rain came pelting down on the roof once again.

"Really?"

Determined to rest, she pulled the covers over her head and willed herself to fall asleep.

CHAPTER NINETEEN

Friday morning dawned bright and clear. Martha rose earliest of all the sisters. Still dressed in her pajamas, she headed down to the kitchen. She couldn't help herself. There was last-minute work to be done, and she was never one to shy away from work. She felt sure everyone who knew her would agree wholeheartedly. Not that she wanted to be known for her work ethic, but right now that shoe fit. Tightly.

When she arrived in the kitchen, she put the coffee on to brew and spent some time praying about the day ahead. If not for the muddy ground and broken tree branches visible through the window, one would never know a storm had raged through the night. The sun rose with such lovely colors that it took Martha's breath away as she gazed upward through the glass. It now motivated her to get to work.

She hummed a familiar worship song as she removed all twelve layers of cake from the refrigerator and began the arduous process of filling and stacking them into four separate tiers. Anna had chosen strawberry preserves for the filling, one of Martha's favorites. But first…buttercream. She whipped up her favorite recipe until it was smooth and creamy, the perfect texture for spreading, then she prepped herself for the construction of the cake.

She started with the twelve-inch cakes, setting the first one on the cake drum, which she'd placed on a handy turntable.

She smoothed on a layer of buttercream. Then she piped a dam around the edge of the cake using the same buttercream, slightly thickened. Afterward, she filled the cake with preserves. Yum.

Martha added the next layer of cake on top of it and repeated the process until the twelve-inch tier was complete. She added a crumb coat of icing to the outside of the cake, added dowels for support, and put it into the fridge. Then she started on the ten-inch layers. When they came together, she turned her attention to the eight-inch cakes, then the six-inch.

By the time she heard her sisters moving around upstairs, Martha had completed all four tiers and had them resting in the refrigerator. Piecing the tiers together and running a long dowel down the center would wait until she arrived at the reception site tomorrow morning. At that point, she would add the greenery and leaves as well. Otherwise, the naked cake was ready to go. Finally.

Content with the outcome, Martha sat at the kitchen table with a cup of coffee and did her best not to fret over the pain in her shoulders and upper back. The pain would go away in time, and seeing the smile on Anna's face tomorrow would make it all worthwhile. Cake baking was tough work, but at least the worst was behind her now.

She spent the next several minutes in prayer, thanking God for seeing her through this storm—both literal and metaphorical.

Mary buzzed into the kitchen a short time later, and her eyes widened. "Oh my goodness. You're already up?"

"You bet. And the cakes are done too. I even did another round of dishes."

"What?" Mary looked genuinely stunned by this news. "But you had all day to get those cakes filled and frosted. Why did you get going so early?"

"Because I knew we need to go to Anna's place today and decorate, and someone has to open the shop."

"What am I, chopped liver?" Elizabeth asked as she entered the room.

Martha laughed. "No, silly. But I think you should go with Mary in my place. There's a lot to do over there, and I know Anna is anxious. I was going to go, but I…" Martha stretched her upper back and sighed. "I need to stay off my feet. I plan to pull a barstool behind the counter at the shop and rest my weary bones. Unless a customer needs me, I mean. Then I'll get up, of course."

"Are you sure, Martha?" Elizabeth did not look convinced. "I'm totally fine to stay here and help you. I don't mind a bit."

Martha shook her head, but the pain in her neck made it difficult, so she stopped. "No, please go help Anna. We promised she'd have two of the three of us there to help. And trust me when I say I can't be one of the two. Not today."

"Okay, if you're sure."

Martha nodded and took another sip from her coffee cup. Gauging from the look on Elizabeth's face, she wasn't altogether sure wedding prep sounded like a lot of fun.

To Elizabeth, wedding prep didn't sound like much fun. But she agreed to go along with Mary to help out because Martha asked her to. If anyone deserved a break today, it was Martha. Her sister looked thrilled to be left behind. After last night's baking adventures, no doubt she was happy to focus on something other than wedding cake.

By ten o'clock, Elizabeth and Mary had loaded the back of the SUV with decor—everything from chalkboards to centerpieces to antique lanterns. As they drove to the Bennett farm, they passed by the Wittmer place. Elizabeth gazed out over the fields ripe for harvest and tried to picture Jackson working alongside his brothers. Perhaps one day he would return—if not for good, then to visit. She ushered up a silent prayer for that very thing.

Mary chattered nonstop about all the things she needed to do once they arrived at the Bennett place, but Elizabeth only heard half of it. She was far too busy thinking about where Jackson may be, how he might be doing after last night's big storm. Hopefully he was okay. Something in her gut told her that he was not, though she wasn't sure why she felt so strongly that he might be in trouble.

Mary pulled the vehicle up to the barn door and backed in. "It'll be easier to empty the back of the car this way," she explained. "And I want to avoid the mud. That's all I need, to coat my shoes in mud. Knowing me, I'll slip and fall."

"Well, if you do, I'll do my best to catch you," Elizabeth said and then laughed. "If I don't fall myself."

It turned out that they had lots of help. Anna's whole family was gathered together, working frantically to convert the old family barn into a beautiful wedding facility. It looked like they were making great strides, but Anna's mother was especially happy to see Mary show up with the rest of the decor.

So was Anna. She sprinted their way, holding tightly to her fiancé's hand. "The rental company just dropped off the tables and chairs, and we're waiting on the caterers to come and set up their serving area. Come and see the cake table, ladies. You're going to flip. Wayne did such a great job. You're not going to believe it!"

Her fiancé's face flamed red, but he didn't argue with her assessment of his work.

She led the way through the maze of tables and chairs to an oversized table near the front of the room. "See what he did?" Anna asked. "Adding the wagon wheels was an amazing idea!"

"Actually, that was your idea, honey," Wayne said with the wave of his hand.

"Well, yes." She giggled. "That's true. But look at the frame he built to hang the chandeliers and lanterns from. Isn't it just perfect? Can't you just picture the cake and other sweets filling up this space, surrounded by flowers and such?"

"It's going to be beautiful," Mary said. "I can picture it now. And Wayne, you did a stellar job. Very rustic."

Elizabeth couldn't help but agree. If this was what farmhouse chic looked like, she was going to love it.

"Do I dare ask how the cake's coming?" Fine lines appeared on Anna's forehead. "I know Martha must've been up all night. And that storm!"

"The cake is all done and chilling in the fridge," Elizabeth explained. "All four tiers. And one day we'll tell you the story about what happened while she was baking it. Let's just say it's one of those stories that will be funnier years from now. For now let's just get busy decorating."

"Of course!" Anna faced Elizabeth. "Elizabeth, can you start by putting the tablecloths on the tables? Then Mary can set up the centerpieces."

"I'd be happy to."

"Mother just finished ironing the tablecloths. You'll find them on hangers at the back of the room. Oh, and we've also got to put seat covers on the chairs." She reached over and squeezed Elizabeth's hand. "Have I mentioned how glad I am that you're here? It's made my day to have you on the team."

"Thank you." She felt her cheeks grow warm. "I'm happy to help, Anna. I'm so excited about your big day. It's going to be beautiful." Her gaze swept the room, and Elizabeth had to admit, all the work that had gone into making Anna's big day perfect would truly pay off in this beautiful setting.

"I'm just so glad that storm is behind us." Anna beamed. "Now everyone can relax and just enjoy the process."

"Right." Still, as Elizabeth got to work, she didn't find herself terribly relaxed. Her thoughts kept shifting back to Jackson Wittmer and to the pained expression on Susanna's face as she'd talked about seeing him return to the fold. More than ever, Elizabeth wanted to play a role in returning the prodigal to those who loved him.

They worked on the decor for a couple of hours, pausing only to take a light lunch around noon. Then they got right back to it. Elizabeth found herself helping the caterers set up their serving station. Not that she minded one bit. No, as the room came together, as she began to see elements of beauty—in the centerpieces, the hanging lights, the flowers—she was completely in awe.

Sometime around three, she paused to stretch her back and check her phone for messages.

"Taking a break?" Mary asked.

Elizabeth nodded. "Yes, my lower back is hurting, probably from bending over so much. I'm not used to this much activity. And it looks like I missed a call from an unfamiliar number."

"Probably one of those telemarketers. You know how they are." Mary walked over to the table where the bridal party would be sitting and fastened a long strand of silk flowers to the front of it.

Elizabeth listened to her messages and was astounded at what she heard. The voice sounded only slightly familiar, and his words held her spellbound.

"Hello, this is Amir Hassan. You came to my station a few nights ago looking for a man who'd gone missing. I wanted to let you know that he came back into my store today to buy something. Not sure where he went after that, but probably not far, because he was on foot. He looked bad. Really bad. Much worse than before. I think he must be very sick. In fact, I really thought he was going to collapse in my store. Thank God he didn't. Just thought you'd want to know."

At that, the message ended.

Elizabeth's hand began to tremble, and she nearly dropped the phone. "Oh my goodness!"

Anna walked her way, crinkles forming around her eyes. "Everything okay, Elizabeth? You're white as a sheet."

"Yes, just something I need to take care of. Quickly. I…I think maybe I have to leave. I wonder if Mary would mind."

A look of panic crossed Anna's face. "But she still has a lot to do. Do you really need her to go with you?"

"No, I...well, I'm sure I can handle this on my own." Before making that decision, she wanted to talk to Mr. Hassan first-hand. Elizabeth punched in his number and waited for him to pick up. When he did, she rushed into the conversation. "Mr. Hassan, this is Elizabeth Classen."

"Oh, yes. You got my message?"

"I did. What time did he come in?"

"About twenty minutes ago. Glad you got back with me so soon."

Elizabeth gasped. "Is he still there?"

"Nah. I sold him a twelve-pack, and he headed out. Like I said, he looks pretty bad. Smelled bad too. I think maybe he's sleeping under one of the bridges near here. There's a community of down-and-outers that camp out on Highway 30 under the New Holland Pike overpass?"

"Even in this weather? It's getting cold out there."

"Yep. Hey, listen, I need to go. I've got customers. Just thought you'd want to know."

"But did you call the police? Do they know that—"

The call ended with a click, and she stared at the phone, dumbfounded.

Mary walked her way, creases forming between her eyes. "You look like you've seen a ghost, Lizzie. Who was that?"

"It was the gas station owner. Jackson was just in his store buying beer."

"Whoa."

Elizabeth brushed her palms on her slacks. "I have no choice, Mary. I have to get over there to see if I can find him. He said Jackson was on foot, so surely he didn't go far. And he also said that Jackson looks ill. Very ill."

Mary's eyes widened. "But we're not done. I can't just leave."

"I'm not asking you to leave, but I have to." Elizabeth reached over and put her hand on Mary's. "You and Martha have worked so hard on this wedding. What I've done is nothing in comparison, and I'm sorry about that. I hate to let you down, but please go on without me."

"It's not a matter of letting me down. The bigger question is whether I'll get anything done after you walk out that door. Do you honestly think I'll be able to focus on the wedding knowing you're out there alone, looking for Jackson? What if something goes wrong? What if he turns out to be a criminal of some sort? What if you encounter someone out on the street who tries to rob you?"

"Your imagination is in overdrive, Mary."

"Maybe, but right now my imagination is what's protecting you." She paused and then snapped her fingers. "I know! I'm going to call John and ask him to go with you."

"O-okay."

"Maybe he'll swing by to pick you up."

"In his patrol car? I don't think so."

As it happened, John was off-duty. He offered to pick Elizabeth up in his personal vehicle and arrived just ten minutes later. She climbed into the passenger seat, and they took off, headed toward Lancaster. John glanced Elizabeth's way and raised his eyebrows. "I hate to bring it up, but you have straw in your hair."

"I do?" She swept her fingers through her hair and came out with a golden piece of hay. "Ack. I must look awful."

"No, you don't. You've been working hard. I can't say that I've ever seen anyone prep for a wedding and locate a missing person on the same day."

"Oh, I do hope we locate him." She glanced at his speedometer. "Can you go a little faster?"

"Um, no. I like to stick to the speed limit, and not just because I'm an officer of the law. And besides, I can only go as fast as the guy in front of me." He gestured to a sedan ahead of them.

She settled back against the seat and tried to calm herself.

"I do have one bit of news," John said.

"Oh?"

"Yes, we were able to check with Jackson's bank—not his mortgage company but his bank—and he made a hefty deposit on Saturday afternoon. In person."

"Whoa. That's great news." She was so relieved to hear the money from the sale of the truck was safe and sound.

"Yes. The bank isn't far from the gas station where he was seen, so I'm guessing he's still in that area."

"Hopefully, but that was days ago. Do you mind if I call Fred Zucker?" she asked. "I want to let him know."

"By all means."

She pulled out her phone and punched in Fred's number. He answered after only a couple of rings.

"Fred, this is Elizabeth Classen. Are you busy? If not, I'd like you to meet me at that gas station. And I need you to bring Rocky."

"Gas station? Why?"

"I've had a call that Jackson was in the store about half an hour ago."

"I'm on my way." She heard him call out to Rocky as he ended the call.

About ten minutes later they pulled into the station. Fred was already there waiting on them. He opened his car door, and Rocky came bounding out. The pooch headed straight for John, almost knocking him over.

Fred took one look at them and hollered, "Well? What are we waiting for? Let's go find my friend."

CHAPTER TWENTY

Unfortunately, they did not find Fred's friend. Despite hours of searching and checking out every restaurant, bridge, and store within a five-mile radius.

Rocky wailed as they slowed the car and put the windows down to examine one location—an underpass beneath Highway 30. Had he picked up on a scent? If so, little good it would do them. The area was vacant, with the exception of a bunch of cardboard boxes and a pile of blankets tossed on the sidewalk. Still, the poor dog was beside himself as they kept driving. So was Fred, who seemed devastated not to find his friend.

They searched until the sun went down, but Jackson was nowhere to be found. Only when they stumbled across an elderly homeless man walking along the edge of the highway did they find any clues at all.

"I think I know the fella yer lookin' fer," the old man drawled after looking at a picture John showed him. "Keeps to himself and moves around a lot, but I've seen 'im." He squinted and gave the picture a closer look. "Don't look much like that anymore though. He's the sickly sort."

Elizabeth rested her hand on the man's arm. "Please keep an eye out for him. We're very worried."

"Sure." The man's gaze shifted to the ground. "Wonderin' what that'd feel like, to know someone was out there, lookin' fer ya. Ain't got nobody on the prowl fer me, guarantee ya." He chuckled. "'Less you count my parole officer."

Elizabeth didn't even know what to say in response. Her eyes welled with tears, but she did what she could to press them away and to push down the lump that had suddenly risen in her throat.

"If you see him," Fred said, "tell him to call his neighbor. Please. And tell him that Rocky misses him something awful."

"Rocky?" The man looked confused.

Fred pointed to the dog, who jumped up and down at the mention of his name.

"Oh, the pooch. Right. Seems like a friendly fella." The man scratched Rocky behind the ears, and a faraway look came over him. "I had a dog once. Real nice one. They ain't called man's best friend fer nuthin'."

"True," Elizabeth said.

"As for this Jackson person calling you, ain't likely he's got a phone. Out here, phones get snatched up in a hurry. But I'll tell 'im if I see 'im."

They thanked the man and then headed back to Bird-in-Hand after dropping Fred off at his car. John promised to call him if they had any news. The poor fellow looked absolutely devastated to be going home alone. So did Rocky, for that matter. It took a bit of nudging to get him into Fred's car.

"Well, that was a sad sight," John said after they pulled away from the gas station. "I feel bad for Fred but even worse for the dog."

"Me too. I don't know that I've ever seen a heartbroken canine before, but I'd definitely have to say Rocky is in mourning."

"I hope he doesn't know something we don't."

"What do you mean?" Elizabeth asked.

John shrugged and kept his focus on the road. "Only that dogs have a weird intuition. Jackson's ill, and I wonder if Rocky thinks he's..." John turned on his signal and changed lanes. "Anyway, we'll keep looking. And I won't give up. In fact, I think I'll go back into the station after I drop you off at home."

John changed the subject to Anna's wedding, and Elizabeth wondered how her sister was getting on at the reception hall. She made a quick call to Mary, who was already at home, having dinner with Martha.

"Did you find Jackson?" Mary asked. "We're on pins and needles over here."

"No, I wish we had...but no."

"Oh." The disappointment in Mary's voice was palpable. "Well, come on home. We've saved dinner for you. I hope you're hungry. Martha made pasta."

"I'm on my way."

Elizabeth ended the call, and they continued the journey back to Bird-in-Hand. She thanked John when he dropped her off.

"Anytime," he responded.

When he backed out of the drive, she couldn't help but feel her shoulders slump forward in defeat. All of that work...for nothing.

"Where are you, Jackson?" she whispered. "Are you all right?"

Elizabeth went inside and had dinner with her sisters, doing her best to put Jackson out of her mind. Mary and

Martha carried on about the upcoming wedding, and Elizabeth knew she should join in, but her heart just wasn't in it, though she did her best to pretend. After dinner she excused herself to go up to her room, where she took a hot shower and then laid out her dress for the following day. She needed to shift gears, to focus on Anna and the wedding.

She climbed into bed but had a hard time sleeping. She kept replaying the events of the day, revisiting the sites they'd been to. The gas station. The street corners. The underpass. The cardboard boxes. The blankets. The weary expressions on the faces of the men and women along the way. How broken they seemed. How hopeless.

How would they ever find Jackson in the midst of it all? Did they even stand a chance? Maybe that man was right. Maybe Jackson didn't have a phone anymore. Maybe someone had stolen it from him. Or maybe he'd simply lost it while in a drunken stupor.

She fell into a fitful sleep and dreamed of homeless men on street corners, all alone, with no one searching for them. The dreams caused a headache, which woke her up early in the morning. She rose and took some aspirin, then climbed back into bed. Before she could fall asleep again, her phone rang.

"Blue Blouse?" Fred's voice greeted her. "We've got a problem."

"Problem?"

"Yep. I don't know how he did it, but Rocky slipped out this morning. He followed me out to get the morning paper and never came back."

Elizabeth sat straight up in bed. "What? The dog is gone?"

"Yes. Happened about forty minutes ago. I would've called sooner, but it's so early, and I didn't want to wake you."

"No, it's okay." She propped up the pillows behind her. "What should we do?"

"Well, I'm gonna go searching for him. Just wanted you to know. I remembered you're the praying sort, so maybe you could say a little prayer while I'm out driving around. That'd help. Pray for some of that divine GPS, if you know what I mean."

"Of course." Elizabeth glanced at the clock. 7:20 a.m. The wedding didn't start for three and a half more hours. Maybe she could...

"You still there?" Fred asked.

"Yes, just thinking I'd like to meet you so you're not searching alone."

"That'd be nice, but I hope you don't think I called with that in mind."

"No, of course not."

"Well, if you're really coming, we'd better make a plan. What say we meet up at the gas station, just like yesterday? I have a feeling Rocky's on the hunt for his owner, so I'm guessing he headed that way."

"Okay." She sat up and swung her legs over the edge of the bed. "Give me about forty-five minutes, and I'll be there."

He responded with "See you soon," and then the line went dead.

Elizabeth rose and slipped into her wedding attire. Her hair and makeup were done in a rush, but Fred wouldn't care about that. Maybe she could do a quick touch-up on the way to the wedding later, if all went well. Oh, how she prayed all would go well.

When she got down to the kitchen, Elizabeth found Mary drinking a cup of coffee and eating scrambled eggs and toast.

"Elizabeth?" Her sister gave her a curious look as she took in her attire and makeup. "The wedding's not until eleven. Why are you dressed so early?"

"I've got to make a run to Lancaster." She quickly explained the situation.

Mary shook her head. "You're really going to go searching for Jackson now…dressed in wedding clothes?"

Elizabeth nodded. "I am. And I think I'd better leave right away, before I chicken out. But I promise to be at the ceremony on time. Please don't worry about that."

"I am worried about that, but I'm more worried about your safety. I'm not keen on you going alone." Mary reached for her phone. "I'm calling John."

"No, please don't. I hate to bother him again, especially this early in the morning. Besides, we'll probably end up at a dead end, just like yesterday."

"Still…" Mary stared at her phone, then back up at Elizabeth. "I don't feel right about you being alone."

"I won't be alone. I'll be with Fred."

Mary set her phone down with a sigh. "That does make me feel a little bit better, but keep your phone handy, and call me if you hear anything. If I don't hear from you within the hour I'm sending the police after you. I'd come after you myself, but I've got to be at the wedding early to help."

"Of course."

Elizabeth climbed behind the wheel of her car and drove as fast as the law would allow to Lancaster. As she made her way down the scenic country roads, she couldn't help but think of Rocky, about how desperately he missed his master. How he longed for nothing more than to sit at Jackson's feet and be close. How he would travel any number of miles to be with him, paying no regard for his own comfort. What a spiritual lesson there was in all of that. She had a lot to learn from that precious pooch. The message did not go unnoticed.

How God must long for his children to sit at His feet, to spend time in His presence. How it must grieve Him when his children wander from the fold. The world was full of prodigals with hearts pointed in every direction...except home.

Elizabeth began to pray in earnest for those in her own circle who had wandered away from the Lord—relatives, friends, and so on. Many had turned their back on their faith in search of seemingly shinier lights. But it wasn't too late. God would search them out and prove His love to them. He would soften their hearts and put them on a path toward healing. And she would stand in the gap and pray until that happened.

After a few minutes she turned her attention to praying for Jackson—for his safety and his heart. No matter what he was going through, she prayed he would come into the safety of a relationship with the Lord. She thought again about that scripture from Psalms, the one about how God placed the lonely in families. No matter what Jackson was going through, God longed for him to return to those who loved him so he could be healed from the pain of the past. That was God's desire for all of His kids, in fact.

Within minutes, she pulled into the parking lot at the gas station, and her cell phone rang. Ack. John. She slipped the car into a parking spot.

"Elizabeth, hope I didn't wake you," he said when she answered. "Just wanted you to know that the updated cell phone records came through just now. There haven't been any calls from Jackson's phone since Monday when he made a call to the mortgage company."

Her nerves kicked in as a couple of men with beer cans in hand drew near her car. "I guess that confirms that he was attempting to cut a last-minute deal to save the house." She double-checked the locks to make sure no one could open her car door. Thankfully, the men passed on by, deep in conversation with each other.

"Likely."

"Do you think the phone was stolen after that?" She watched as an older-model sedan pulled into the spot next to her. Fred Zucker. Knowing he was nearby brought a certain degree of comfort.

"If so, the thief didn't use it, which leads me to believe the battery died. I do see that Fred Zucker tried to reach him repeatedly over the past several days. He never stopped trying."

"Well, speaking of Fred..." She paused and looked out the window, where a very animated Fred was trying to get her attention. "He just pulled up. I'm meeting him in Lancaster."

"You're...what?" John groaned. "And here I thought I woke you up. What are you doing over in Lancaster?"

"Rocky ran away this morning, and Fred is out searching for him. I decided to join him."

"I'll be there in twenty minutes."

"No, you really don't need to do that, John. If we find Rocky I'll leave him with Fred and come straight back to the wedding. I'll just see you there. Please don't worry."

"Too late."

He ended the call, and she shoved her phone into her purse then got out of her car to find a very excited Fred Zucker.

"I think we're in luck," he said. "Remember that man we talked to yesterday? He came walking out of the station and recognized me. Told me he'd seen Rocky a few blocks from here, just under the bridge on 30."

"Really?" Elizabeth hated to get her hopes up, but found herself excited. "Hop in my car, Fred. Let's go find him."

He gave her an inquisitive look. "Don't you think you're a little overdressed for the occasion?"

"Oh." She glanced down at her dress and jewelry. "I'm headed to a wedding after this."

"Are you a bridesmaid?"

"No." She laughed. "Hardly. My friend is getting married, and I just want to look nice."

"Well, you've accomplished that goal. But out here on the streets you look a mite out of place."

They headed back to the same sites they'd visited yesterday. When they rounded the corner where they'd seen the cardboard boxes, Fred let out a whoop. "There he is! There's Rocky! Ah, I knew we'd find him."

Elizabeth tapped the brakes and slowed the car as they passed under the freeway. There, on the side of the road, the dog lay huddled next to the same pile of blankets she'd seen yesterday. Even from here, she could tell Rocky was in distress.

There was no place to park, so she had to circle the street again, this time pulling to a stop in a nearby church parking lot. She and Fred both hurried from the car in the direction of the bridge. They arrived to find Rocky pressed up against the blankets, wailing. Fred took hold of the pooch's collar and tried to calm him, but the dog would not be silenced. He nudged at the pile of blankets, clearly frantic. Elizabeth gently lifted the edge of the torn blanket on top of the pile, and her breath caught in her throat.

Jackson Wittmer.

And he didn't appear to be breathing.

CHAPTER TWENTY-ONE

O h, no!" Elizabeth pulled the blankets off Jackson. "Fred, call 911!" As he reached for his phone, she started checking for a pulse. For a moment she couldn't find one. Then Jackson stirred. Ever so slightly, he moved, and hope surged through her veins. He was still alive…for now.

"Stay with me, Jackson." Elizabeth tried to steady her voice. "Don't give up. We're here now. Fred is here. And Rocky."

In the background, she could hear Fred talking to the 911 dispatcher. Then a barrage of questions came from the other end of the line: "Is he breathing? Can he speak? Does he appear to have fallen?"

"He's breathing," Elizabeth said. "But barely. I don't know the answers to the other questions. Please tell them to hurry."

She knelt down on the sidewalk and tucked a blanket under Jackson's head. He looked awful. His skin was a deep amber color, and he was thinner than before. All but his belly, which was huge. He reeked—a combination of smells nearly knocked her over—but that was the least of her worries. He was burning up with fever and sweating, in spite of the coolness in the air.

A couple of minutes later, she heard the sound of the sirens approaching. To her right, Fred was making another phone call to someone else. She couldn't be sure who, but his words were frantic, choppy.

Just as the paramedics arrived, John pulled up in his patrol car. He bounded from the car and rushed their way.

"Is he—"

"He's alive." Elizabeth couldn't help herself. She burst into tears, now bent over Jackson.

"We need you to step back, ma'am." The paramedic's firm voice nudged her away from the scene. She rose and took several steps away from Jackson and watched as they took his vitals then listened closely as one paramedic called out the information to the other: "Blood pressure 89/55. Acute swelling of the abdomen. Jaundice. Temperature 103.7. Let's load 'im, guys. We need to get an IV started to knock this fever down then get him to the hospital."

The second paramedic unloaded the gurney from the ambulance, and the two men worked together to lift Jackson's frail body onto it. Elizabeth kept her distance until they had Jackson in the back of the vehicle. Then she had to ask the obvious question. "Is he going to be okay?"

"Ma'am, what's your relationship to the patient?"

"Oh, I—"

"Are you a relative?"

Elizabeth shook her head. "No. I'm just an acquaintance."

"I'm family." A frantic female voice sounded from behind her. Elizabeth turned and saw that a young woman had joined them. Her eyes were wide and frantic. Elizabeth recognized her right away.

Emily.

"I'm his wife. Er, ex-wife." Emily reached into the ambulance and grabbed Jackson's hand. "Is he okay?"

The paramedic glanced her way. "Based on the size of his abdomen I'm guessing he's in acute liver failure, but he's stable. Do you know if he has a history of Hep C?"

"Not that I know of."

Fred cleared his throat. "He's been drinking a lot more than normal lately. I know that."

The paramedic nodded. "Could be alcohol poisoning. We've got to get going, *stat*. Can you follow us to Lancaster General? Maybe answer a few more questions when we get there?"

"Yes." Emily turned toward her car. "I'll meet you in the ER."

The paramedic hurried to the front of the ambulance and climbed inside.

Emily turned to face them. She gave Fred a big hug. "Thank you for calling me. I've been worried sick about him."

"Me too. Thanks for coming, Emily."

Emily glanced Elizabeth's way, and Elizabeth introduced her to John.

"Henri told me you've been looking for Jackson for days." Emily squeezed Elizabeth's hand. "I can't thank you enough. I've been worried sick, ever since I got the news he was missing. Something told me he'd stopped his treatments, and I knew that going without them could be deadly." Tears flooded her eyes. "I pray he's been found in time to turn things around. If so, we have you to thank." She threw her arms around Elizabeth and gave her a tight squeeze. Seconds later, she climbed back in her car and followed the ambulance as it pulled away from the scene.

Fred stood with Rocky at his side, looking completely shell-shocked, his eyes misted over with tears. "I had no idea."

"Me neither. But I guess it explains the dark tan."

"Yes, he was completely jaundiced," John said.

"I...I..." Fred pressed his palm against his forehead, unable to speak for a moment. "It's my fault. I should've offered to take him in."

"No, you've done so much for him already," Elizabeth said. "You're a good friend."

"A good friend would've kept him from landing under a bridge. I can't believe he felt this was his only option."

"You can't blame yourself, Fred," John said. "You went above and beyond."

"I just can't understand why he wouldn't have told me he was ready to give up on life like this. I would've done something, said something..."

"No doubt he was in shock over losing the house," Elizabeth said. "And being so sick probably affected his ability to think clearly, especially if he'd stopped taking his treatments. You know?"

"Right." Fred's expression brightened. "I'll be a better friend from now on. This will never happen again, not while I'm around. I'll take good care of him."

Elizabeth looked at her phone and gasped when she saw the time. Ten fifteen.

"Oh, no! Speaking of going, I'm going to miss the wedding if I don't get on the road. Let me get you back to your car, Fred, and then I'll be on my way."

"I'll drop him off," John said. "Then I'll meet you at the ceremony. You go ahead and hit the road, Elizabeth. I'd hate to see you miss Anna's big day."

Elizabeth walked back to her car and got inside. She made a quick call to Mary, but there was no answer. No doubt she was helping with last-minute details for the wedding. A call to Martha went unanswered too. Likely she was setting up the cake, even now. Oh well. She would see them soon enough. Right now she needed to call Susanna. Using the Bluetooth feature in her car, she made the call while she drove toward Bird-in-Hand.

Thank goodness, Susanna answered the phone.

"We've found him, Susanna." Relief flooded over her, even as she spoke the words aloud. "We've found Jackson."

"What? You have? I was just making some calls trying to locate him. That is why you caught me in the phone shack. Is he all right?"

"He's stable."

"Where was he, Elizabeth? What happened to him?"

"I'll let Emily fill you in when you see her. The ambulance is on its way to the hospital in Lancaster if you want to meet them there."

"I cannot thank you enough for doing this for our family, Elizabeth."

"You're welcome. But, Susanna, before you see him, I think you should know that Jackson is suffering from complications of liver disease. Likely alcohol poisoning."

"Liver disease?" Susanna's voice tightened. "Are you sure?"

"Yes, you'll have to ask Emily for more details when the timing is right. Apparently it was a bigger problem than anyone knew."

"I have to believe this is why Jackson stayed away. He knew Daed would know and be upset."

"Maybe."

"I'm glad Jackson did not let Daed see him like that, to be honest. It would have been too much to handle on top of what he was already going through. Daed's last hours were peaceful." She paused. "Though, I have to tell you, it broke my heart when Jackson did not show up for Daed's funeral. But maybe that is why he chose to bring the pitcher to your shop. Maybe he could not stay away. Maybe he was just looking for an excuse to come back one last time."

"I'm guessing you're right, Susanna. It is probably more than a coincidence that Jackson showed up right after your father passed. I hadn't thought about it, but it makes perfect sense."

The conversation shifted back to Jackson's current condition, and then Susanna said her goodbyes. "We need to get on the road to the hospital, Elizabeth. You relax and enjoy the wedding. Please give the bride my best wishes."

"I will."

With her heart in her throat, Elizabeth finished the drive to Bird-in-Hand. Her thoughts tumbled in a thousand different directions. She pondered Jackson's situation, then spent time praying earnestly—for his healing and for his relationship with Emily. Elizabeth couldn't help but think that God was up to something here. She also couldn't help but think that the Lord had a greater message for her, a calling to pray for people more fervently, to love them more deeply, in spite of their struggles.

She pulled up to the Bennett farm at ten forty-five, with fifteen minutes to spare. A quick glance in the rearview mirror revealed messy hair and smeared mascara. She did her best to fix her hair and touch up her makeup, then climbed out of the car and walked inside the barn, which was teeming with happy wedding-goers. Overhead, lovely instrumental music played a familiar love song. Elizabeth looked around for her sisters and finally located them at a table near the front. They had saved her a seat.

She found herself completely mesmerized by the sheer beauty of the room. The bales of hay, all the burlap...it made perfect sense now. So did the mason jars and lace. The whole thing was complete perfection.

"Well?" Mary asked.

"We found him."

"What? Oh my goodness, tell us everything."

She did her best to fill them in. Mary and Martha looked genuinely shocked to hear about Jackson's condition.

"That's awful." Mary shook her head. "I can't even imagine what would have happened to him if you hadn't listened to the Lord and gone when you did."

"I thought about that too," Elizabeth said. "I don't think he would have lasted much longer. I really don't." Her eyes filled with tears, and she brushed them away. "I'm just so glad he's in good hands now. That's what he needs more than anything—people who care."

"True," Martha agreed. "And I'm so happy to hear that Emily is with him too."

"Yes, we have Fred to thank for that. He called her, and she came right away."

"Sounds like the lost sheep has been returned to the fold," Mary said.

"Lost sheep." Elizabeth repeated the words aloud. "Funny you should say that. I've been thinking about all of the Jacksons in my world. There are a lot of broken people out there, and sometimes I drive right past them. They're there, under bridges and on street corners. But they're also in our churches, sitting alone in pews on Sunday mornings. They don't want to bother others with their personal woes, so they stay quiet."

"That's true, Elizabeth." Mary nodded.

"It breaks my heart to think that some people have nowhere to turn, no one to listen. God never designed us to walk alone. You know? He's so good to give us each other."

"Well, of course He is." Martha slipped her arm over Elizabeth's shoulders.

"The Bible says He places the lonely in families. I think that's in Psalms somewhere. He places people in groups of loving, caring people so they're not alone. He gave Jackson a family when he planted him next door to Fred."

"And even Rocky as a member of his family," Mary added.

"Right. But I've been thinking about the Wittmers, how they found a long-lost brother. God has placed Jackson in that family too. They have each other to bring comfort after losing a loved one." Elizabeth's eyes filled with tears, and she felt a lump ease its way into her throat. "And I have you. After Mama's death I wondered if I'd be sitting alone in that big house—just me and Pal. But I'm not alone. God placed me in a family, and He made sure I had people."

"So true," Martha said. "And this conversation reminds me of Anna. She was so lonely before she met Wayne. I know she had a job that kept her busy and all, but I can't tell you how many phone calls and texts I got from her over the years. She felt sure she would never fit in anywhere. Now she's got her own little family—a new husband and his two grown children."

Elizabeth's heart filled with joy as she thought about how the Lord had orchestrated all of that. "So many people come and go from our shop on a regular basis. Many don't really have families. They're loners. I'm going to pay more attention to them and reach out to them, make sure they don't feel overlooked. I'm just feeling a nudge from the Lord to be more inclusive and to make people feel like they've been swept into the fold when they come into the store. Does that make sense?"

"I love your heart, Elizabeth," Mary said. "You're always looking out for the underdog, and I love that about you."

"I think God has just awakened my heart to lonely people," Elizabeth explained. "I want to show them how much I care."

"You already do." Mary offered her sister a warm smile. "And trust me when I say that people notice. In fact, it's one of the things they love most about you."

The music shifted to Pachelbel's Canon in D and intensified in volume. A few seconds later the groom-to-be and his groomsmen entered the barn, dressed in tuxedos. Elizabeth shifted her thoughts to the wedding. In this moment, nothing mattered more than Anna and her big day.

CHAPTER TWENTY-TWO

Elizabeth had a wonderful time at the wedding but was equally glad the event was behind them. Now her sisters could relax and get back to their normal routines. October was more than halfway gone now, and the fall season was in full swing with pumpkins and gourds making appearances at every turn. She and her sisters went to church on Sunday, then rested that afternoon. By Monday morning she was ready to get back to work at the shop. Only, her sisters had other plans, which they announced as soon as she took her place behind the register.

"Oh no you don't!" Mary scolded.

"Don't what?"

"It's your birthday, Elizabeth! You're not working today."

"Wait. It...it is?" She paused to think it through, then grinned as the realization set in. "With all the craziness of the weekend, I forgot! Who forgets her own birthday?"

"You, apparently." Mary laughed. "But who could blame you? Things have been a little crazy around here lately."

"True. We have been a little busy, what with the wedding, the crime-solving, and all," Martha added. "But today is definitely your big day, and we want you to pamper yourself."

"Yes, go for a pedicure," Mary suggested. "Or get a massage. But get out of here, and let us do the work."

Such a notion seemed foreign to Elizabeth. "Are you kidding me? Get a pedicure...without the two of you? I wouldn't know what to do with myself. Who would I talk to?"

"No one!" Martha laughed again. "Rest. Relax. Take some time to yourself to think, to pray, to just...be."

"I love you for thinking that might sound appealing," Elizabeth admitted. "But in all honesty, I'd rather curl up with a good book than have my toenails painted."

"Then curl up with a good book while you're getting your toenails painted," Mary suggested. "But, seriously, we just want you to enjoy your day. We've got a big dinner planned, so make sure you come home hungry."

"And I'm making a birthday cake—your favorite, Italian cream cake," Martha added. "It's going to be so yummy."

"Are you serious?" Elizabeth was flabbergasted that Martha would even consider such a thing. "After that huge wedding cake you just baked? I couldn't ask you to do that."

"I've already got the ingredients, and there's no way you're talking me out of it. So scoot on out of here, and don't let me catch you peeking in my kitchen while I'm working. I want the design to be a surprise."

"Everything you do is a surprise, Martha. Have I mentioned how floored I was by that beautiful wedding cake?"

"Well, all the hard work was definitely worth it," Martha said. "I think it came out great, even if it was naked."

"You really outdid yourself, Martha," Mary agreed. "And I know that Anna loved it. She raved over it. In fact, I think she was pleased with everything, including all of the decor. But she only had eyes for her groom, and that's how it should have been."

Elizabeth couldn't help but smile as her sisters lit into a conversation about Anna's big day. "I still say you're a wonder, Martha. Truly."

"The only 'wonder' here is me wondering if you're gonna skedaddle and take a day off." Martha grinned. "Go on. Shoo."

"Okay, okay." Elizabeth collected her purse and walked toward the exit. Before she could make it, a familiar man walked through the front door, arms loaded with boxes. She couldn't help but grin when she saw Fred Zucker standing there.

"Well, I've waited long enough, ladies. But I'm here now." He set the boxes down on the counter.

"Waited long enough?" Elizabeth slung her purse strap over her shoulder. "What do you mean?"

"I mean, I've finally started clearing out that house of mine. Downsizing."

"Really?" Mary came alongside Elizabeth and rested her hand on one of the boxes. "That's awesome, Fred."

He paused and then pointed at her blouse. "That's the same pink blouse you were wearing the first day I met you."

"Is it?" Mary glanced down and shrugged. "I didn't realize."

"Yep." He turned to Elizabeth. "And you were dressed in blue."

"I was indeed."

Fred grinned. "Anyway, I figured what better place to bring all of my stuff than your shop? I think it'll fetch a good price. Most of it, anyway. The more expensive stuff'll sell online, but there's enough merchandise in the back of my truck to fill several shelves. You did say you take things on consignment, right?"

"Sure do," Elizabeth said. "And I'll be happy to take a look."

"Great. 'Cause I've got three more boxes of stuff in the back of the truck. I'll fetch it when you're done looking through this stuff. Don't want to overwhelm you."

"Not overwhelmed at all. We're tickled to have more merchandise. People really start shopping for Christmas at this time of year."

Mary shot her a "Aren't you supposed to be headed home to read a book?" look, but Elizabeth didn't respond. How could she resist going through these boxes?

They opened the first one, and Martha joined them. "You've got some wonderful pieces here," she said. "These will bring in a pretty penny."

Fred looked pleased. "Thanks. I hope so. I plan to use some of that money to help Jackson out."

Elizabeth gasped. "Really?"

"Yep. Can't think of a thing I'd rather do with it. And besides, who needs all this stuff, anyway? It's so pointless."

"Speaking of Jackson, how is he doing?" Mary asked. "Last we heard, he was on the upswing."

"Doc said it was alcohol poisoning, all right, but they caught it in time and got him back on his feet in a hurry. It was miraculous how fast they got him turned around. Now we just need to keep him there."

Elizabeth's heart swelled with joy that God had led them to Jackson before it was too late.

Fred waved his hand in the air. "You know what they say about hindsight being twenty-twenty. I think I must've noticed some of the symptoms all along—his skin was kind of a golden color. I figured he'd been in the sun too much. And he was always complaining about swelling in his ankles and feet. Turns out, that's another symptom. And he got sick to his stomach a lot. I'd noticed some weight loss but figured he was just depressed from losing Emily and Sophia. You know?"

"Right." Elizabeth weighed her next words carefully. "I have to confess, I thought he looked pretty ragged the first time I saw him. Wouldn't have guessed alcoholism, but he looked pretty beaten down by life."

"He has been. But that's what friends are for, right? To lift you back up when you've been beaten down?"

"Right."

"From what I can gather, depression can affect everything, from your health to your mental state. So I'm not surprised he ended up under that bridge. Probably plenty of men—and women—living under bridges are struggling with the very same thing."

"Probably," Elizabeth agreed.

Fred pounded his fist into his other hand. "But I'm not going to let Jackson become a statistic, and neither is that family of his."

"Oh? You met his family?"

"Sure did." Fred's eyes lit up. "They're pretty great, by the way. Still can't get over the fact that Jackson was raised Amish. Who woulda thunk it? Crazy."

"His father was a bishop," Martha said as she pulled items from one of the boxes. "Did you know that part?"

"The sister told me. She's a peach. I really like her. As a matter of fact, she's headed here right now. We're going to grab lunch at some little place she told me about—Two Bird Café."

"One of my favorites," Elizabeth said.

He pointed at her. "Well, you should join us, then. I'm sure Susanna would be tickled pink, and I know I would."

"Oh, do it, Elizabeth!" Mary said.

"It's her birthday," Martha was quick to add.

"Happy birthday to you, Blue Blouse," Fred said. "Now you have no choice. I'm going to treat you to lunch for your birthday."

"I would hate to intrude, especially if you've already got plans with Susanna."

"No intrusion." He grinned. "We'd love to have you. And if anyone deserves celebrating, it's you. You saved my friend's life, you know."

"I'm not sure I'd go that far," she said.

"Well, I'm sure Jackson would love to see you again. Why don't you follow me on outside and ask him yourself how he feels about you joining us."

"What?" She almost lost her breath. "He's here?"

"Yep. Just got released. I stopped by the hospital to pick him up on my way. So come on out. I need to get the rest of those boxes anyway."

Elizabeth practically sprinted to the door. Her breath caught in her throat as she looked through the glass and noticed the red Ford F-150. "Oh, Fred!"

His lips curled up in a delighted grin. "I couldn't help myself. I had to buy it back for him. That's the real reason I'm selling off my stuff, to pay myself back."

"You're serious? You actually bought Jackson's truck?"

"Yep. And I'm giving it back to him. When he's well enough to drive, I mean. Until then, he'll see it sitting in his driveway every day, and it will give him a reason to keep hoping, to keep fighting."

"How much did Chester charge you?" She opened the front door and stepped through onto the parking lot.

"Well, funny you should ask. He paid Jackson $7000 for the truck and then changed the oil and rotated the tires. I offered him $7500, and he took it."

"Whoa."

"Yeah, I just told him what was going on with Jackson. Turns out, he's got a conscience. And it didn't hurt that I took Officer Marks with me. He's a good man."

"He is," Elizabeth agreed as they took a few steps together toward the red truck. "I'm glad you're getting to know him. Though, to be honest, I'm more surprised Chester didn't talk John into buying a new car."

"He tried. But we held our ground and came away with a beautiful red truck, one that was only driven to church on Sundays by a little old lady." Fred doubled over in laughter. His expression grew more serious, and he lowered his voice as he spoke his final thoughts on the matter. "But, hey…please don't say anything to Jackson about it, okay? He wanted to pay me back but I told him to use the money Chester paid him to save his house."

"Isn't it too late?"

"He's got a meeting with the bank on Thursday. I'm hoping they'll work out some sort of plan."

"Wow, that's wonderful." She turned her attention to Jackson, who sat in the front passenger seat. He waved to her through the open window.

"Hey, you!" she called out as she took several steps in his direction.

"Good to see you again," he responded. "Hope you don't mind if I stay put in the car. I'm still a little weak."

He might be weak, but he looked a sure sight better than the last time she'd seen him. Elizabeth wanted to burst into tears, she was so happy. "I don't mind at all."

She turned as she heard the voices of her sisters behind her. They both came rushing toward the truck and introduced themselves. Jackson seemed a little surprised by all of the attention but engaged them in easy conversation.

"Wait, who's manning the shop?" Elizabeth asked as another vehicle pulled into the parking lot.

"Me!" Martha raised her hand and then shot inside ahead of the incoming guests. Mary spoke a few more words to Jackson then went back in as well. Fred busied himself getting another couple of boxes from the back of the truck, but Elizabeth held her place at the passenger window. She'd waited too long for this.

"You look good, Jackson. Really good."

"I'm feeling better. Much better." He shook his head, and a hint of tears rose to cover his lashes. "Speaking of which, I really don't know how to thank you, Ms. Classen."

"Please. No thanks necessary. And call me Elizabeth."

"No, really. The doctor said if you hadn't shown up when you did, I might not be here. I owe you my life."

Her heart felt as if it swelled into her throat as she heard those words. "Well, let's give the Lord credit for that one, shall we? He gave me quite the nudge to look for you on Saturday morning."

"I'm glad you paid attention." Jackson wiped his eyes with the back of his hand. "But Fred told me you were looking for me all along. Is that right?"

"Yes, because of that pitcher you sold me. When I found out it was worth much more than I paid you, I felt it was only right to track you down."

"Yes, Susanna told me that she's got it now. Thank you."

"You're welcome. And I'm glad to hear you've been in touch with your family. They've been so worried."

"Yeah." He raked his fingers through his hair. "Me too. It was too long. The whole thing was…complicated."

She said softly, "I'm sorry about your dad, Jackson. Everyone around here loved him."

"Thank you." His words hung in the air, and Elizabeth wondered if she'd struck a nerve.

She cleared her throat and then thought of a change in conversation. "I'm guessing you're eager to see Rocky."

"Can't wait. He's back at Fred's place."

Fred passed by them, arms full. "You just sit tight, Jackson," he said. "I've got another couple of loads to take in, but it won't take me long."

"Sorry I can't help." Jackson shrugged.

"Don't even think about it. You just sit tight."

Elizabeth decided she'd better get back inside, so she patted Jackson on the arm and told him she would be praying for him. His eyes grew moist once again.

She didn't blame him. In fact, she felt like crying herself as she walked back into the store. Elizabeth found Fred at the front register, opening the boxes with Martha's and Mary's help.

"Fred, thank you for bringing Jackson with you."

"Didn't really have a choice. I was on my way to you when the call came through that he was ready to be picked up."

"It's just so good to see him looking better." She paused. "He seems in pretty good spirits too."

"Well, there's a reason for that." Fred looked her way, and one of his brows elevated. "You'll never guess who's been at the hospital day and night."

"Emily?" Elizabeth and her sisters spoke in unison.

"You're good guessers. She might be his ex, but I guess she's still got feelings for him. In fact, she's going with him to the meeting at the bank. That warms my heart. I don't have a soul who'd step in and take care of me, if I were in a similar position."

His words pricked Elizabeth's heart. She decided in that moment that she would continue to stay in touch with Fred Zucker and make sure he felt included.

"Do you hold out any hope for the two for them?" Mary asked as she pulled items out of the boxes.

"I guess that all depends on Jackson. He's got some tough choices ahead of him. We'll see if he's able to lay down the drinking and change his thinking." Fred laughed. "There I go again, making a rhyme."

"Don't give up on him," Mary said. "I've seen lives turned around. I've seen marriages restored. It could happen."

"Anything's possible with God," Elizabeth added. "But if I were in her shoes I'd want to make absolutely sure he was clean and sober before I'd even consider it. Still, I do believe that everyone deserves a second chance."

"Speaking of second chances, did you see the article in the paper about Chester's Autos?" Fred asked as he reached his hand down into one of the boxes to retrieve something.

"Yes," Elizabeth answered. "Just this morning. I can't believe they recanted their story. You rarely see a paper do that."

"Right?" He pulled a model airplane out of the box and set it on the counter.

"I have to admit, I was happy to see Chester exonerated. Henri was right about him all along."

"Henri? Who's Henri?" Fred's nose wrinkled in obvious confusion.

"I'll tell you all about her over lunch. She's an awesome young woman. Very handy too."

"Hmm. Okay, then. Henri's a her. I'll take your word for it. Let me grab the final box. Be back in a jiff." Fred walked to the back of the truck and returned moments later with another box. Susanna Wittmer entered behind him, all smiles.

"Good morning, friends," she called out as she took a few steps in their direction. "Did you all see my baby brother sitting out there looking so well? Is this not the best day ever?"

They all spoke over each other with their positive responses.

"We've been praying nonstop," Mary added.

"Do not stop." Susanna reached to rest her hand on her arm. "Those prayers are working."

Fred scratched his head and looked back and forth between them. "You people sure pray a lot. Don't know that I've ever met so many praying people."

"That's where the answers are," Elizabeth explained.

Fred looked more perplexed than ever.

"You don't have Rocky with you today, Mr. Zucker?" Susanna asked.

"Nope. I love that big dope, but he's a handful. Besides, I was afraid he'd take off on me. He really seems to like this part of the county."

"I found out why," Susanna said. "Jackson told me that he came over here to Bird-in-Hand at least two or three times a week and brought the dog every time."

"Really?" Elizabeth asked. This certainly took her by surprise.

"Yes. He said he drove by the farm more times than he could count. He said he would get out of the car and walk with Rocky for miles, hoping he could catch a glimpse of us. Would you believe he even said that he watched my brothers plow the land and saw me hanging up clothes on the line?"

"Wow, I'm surprised no one in the family recognized him," Mary said.

Susanna shook her head. "He told me he kept his baseball cap and sunglasses on. He thought we would think he was a stranger, an Englischer. But it does make me wonder how many times I saw my own brother and did not realize it."

"Still can't get over the fact that Jackson grew up Amish." Fred shook his head. "Just can't picture it."

"He did," Susanna said. "And I think a piece of his heart is still here. For sure, a piece of Rocky's heart is here. Jackson said the dog loves this area. I guess that is why he ventured this way when Jackson went missing."

"Poor pup." Martha looked up from her work. "But that would explain it, I guess."

Mary gave Elizabeth a stern look. "What are you still doing here? Didn't we give you orders to celebrate your birthday in style?"

"Oh, is it your birthday?" Susanna offered her a warm smile. "How wonderful."

"Yes, and I invited her to join us for lunch," Fred said. "That is, if you don't mind, Susanna."

"I do not mind a bit. I will take any bit of time I can get with my friends, old and new. And I know Jackson will love getting to know you better, Elizabeth."

"Thank you." She nodded. "If you're sure I won't be in the way."

"You will not be in the way."

"Wait, did Susanna just call me old?" Fred chuckled and then slapped his knee. "Oh well."

Susanna looked back and forth between the sisters and Fred. Her eyes flooded with tears. "I am just so happy to have all of you in my life during this season. You have all been such a blessing."

"I've been called a great many things in my life," Fred said. "But never a blessing."

"Well, you are." Susanna gazed at him with such tenderness that Elizabeth wondered if he might be reduced to tears. "Your sense of humor reminds me so much of my daed."

Fred wrinkled his nose. "Well, I'll have to be honest—I've never been compared to an Amish bishop before. Guess I'll take that as a compliment."

"You should," Susanna said. "You are very much like him in so many ways."

"Well, then, I thank you."

Susanna rested her hand on Fred's arm. "Most of all, I just want to say thank you for adopting my brother over the past several months. I know he has been in a rough place, but you have been there for him every step of the way, and we are so grateful. I am just sorry it took us so long to get involved."

"No need to thank me." Fred's face flamed red. "That's what friends do."

"As far as we are concerned, you went above and beyond. You have given us our brother back, Mr. Zucker. The lost son has returned to the fold. We are so grateful for that."

Fred looked away, as if embarrassed.

Elizabeth's heart was filled with kindness for the man as she asked, "Are you okay?"

He nodded and then looked directly at her. "All that stuff about Jackson returning to the fold just reminded me of a story I heard once as a kid. I guess it was a Bible story, now that I think of it."

"The prodigal son?" Elizabeth asked.

His eyes lit with recognition. "Yes, I think so. Something about the father killing a fatted calf to celebrate when the son came home again? Is that right?"

"Yes, when the son returned home, the father threw an amazing party for him," Elizabeth said. "In fact, heaven throws a big party for all prodigals when they return home."

"Well, I'll be." Fred shook his head. "Guess they're throwing a whopper up there right now, since Jackson's back in the fold and all."

As Elizabeth surveyed the joy on Susanna's face, she had to conclude that heaven was, indeed, throwing a whopper of a party right now. And, if such a thing could be gauged from the peaceful look on Fred Zucker's face, there were plenty more parties to come.

ABOUT THE AUTHOR

Award-winning author Janice Thompson got her start in the industry writing screenplays and musical comedies for the stage. Janice has published over 110 books for the Christian market, crossing genre lines to write cozy mysteries, historicals, romances, nonfiction books, devotionals, children's books, and more. She particularly enjoys writing lighthearted, comedic tales because she enjoys making readers laugh.

Janice is passionate about her faith and does all she can to share the joy of the Lord with others, which is why she particularly enjoys writing. Her tagline, "Love, Laughter, and Happily Ever Afters!" sums up her take on life.

She lives in Spring, Texas, where she leads a rich life with her family, a host of writing friends, and three mischievous pups. When she's not busy writing or playing with her nine grandchildren, Janice can be found in the kitchen, baking specialty cakes and cookies for friends and loved ones. No matter what she's cooking up—books, cakes, cookies, or mischief—she does her best to keep the Lord at the center of it all.

MORE TO THE STORY

Losing Yourself in a Maze

If you've ever had the desire to lose yourself, there's no finer place to do it than in a Lancaster County corn maze. These family-friendly mazes are cut into a field of corn. You will start on one end and come out on the other, likely getting lost at several points along the way in the various dead ends and side trails. Most of the farms will offer a map. You'll have stopping points where you can check off your map along the way.

Most of these mazes are set up on farms that provide other activities for families as well. Whether you're looking for good food (roasted corn, candied apples, whoopie pies, and more), a pumpkin patch, wagon rides, tractor rides, or wholesome entertainment, you'll find it at several family-friendly farms in Lancaster County in the fall.

FRESH FROM MARTHA'S KITCHEN

Tiered Wedding Cake

INGREDIENTS (This recipe will make three 6-inch layers of cake. To make a full wedding cake you will need to multiply this recipe by ten. Yep, you read that right!)

CAKE:

1 15.25-ounce box white cake mix
½ cup oil
4 egg whites

1 cup plus 2 tablespoons water
1 teaspoon clear vanilla
1 teaspoon pure almond extract

Mix cake as per instructions on box, substituting four egg whites instead of three whole eggs. Add vanilla and almond. Bake in three 6-inch pans. Allow to cool on wire racks, then level cakes off in preparation for stacking.

FROSTING:

1 8-ounce block cream
cheese

2 sticks (one cup) butter

1 cup Crisco shortening (white)

1 bag powdered sugar
(7 to 8 cups, sifted)

1 teaspoon clear vanilla
extract

1 teaspoon pure almond
extract

1 to 2 tablespoons Italian
sweet cream creamer

While cakes are baking, allow butter and cream cheese to come to room temperature. When they are ready, whip them for 2 to 3 minutes then add shortening. Turn mixer down to low speed and carefully add 7 to 8 cups of powdered sugar until frosting reaches desired creamy consistency. Add extracts until fully incorporated.

FILLING:

1 18-ounce jar strawberry preserves

INSTRUCTIONS: See Author's Note below.

A NOTE FROM THE AUTHOR

I loved adding the scene where Martha bakes the wedding cake because I've been in her shoes more times than I can count! I love to bake and have done plenty of wedding cakes over the years. With that in mind, I thought it might be fun to tell you a little more about my baking process.

Let's Make a Wedding Cake!
Most people are surprised to learn that my cake recipe (listed above) begins with a boxed mix. To give wedding cake that amazing "Just Married!" flavor, I add both vanilla and almond extracts. You'll notice that I use *only* egg whites instead of whole eggs. This keeps this cake a pristine white. Some folks substitute butter for oil, but I love that bright white color, so oil is just fine for me. When baking in large pans (12-inch diameter or larger) I usually lower the temperature of the oven. If the recipe calls for 350 degrees, I'll lower the temperature to 335 and cook the cakes a bit longer. I also rotate the cakes on the racks of my oven to ensure equal baking. For a typical three-tiered wedding cake, I start with three 6-inch round cake pans, three 9-inch round cake pans, and three 12-inch round cake pans. I bake my cakes until they are golden in color (timing them according to the directions on the cake box) then turn them out to cool on cooling racks. At this point I have a total of nine

cakes. It's important to cool your cake layers completely before decorating. Mine sit out for a couple of hours then go into the fridge to chill.

My Tiering Tools

I have several tools on hand before stacking and tiering my wedding cakes. A good turntable is a must-have. It makes the stacking and decorating process so much easier. I use a sturdy cake drum (foil-covered board at least ¾-inch thick) to build the cake on. I've been known to make my own out of cake rounds, but they can be purchased online as well. The key here is to have a strong base. Each tier will have its own "round" (a cardboard cutout the same size as the cakes on that tier). I usually dowel my layers with Boba (milkshake) straws or wooden dowels. Of course, I also use an offset spatula for adding that yummy icing!

My Tiering Process

I start by placing my cake drum on the turntable. I level off my three 12-inch cakes and begin the process of stacking and filling them. I always make sure I have plenty of frosting and fruit filling on hand. There's nothing worse than running short midway through the stacking process! Many of my wedding cakes have a fruit filling between the layers, most often strawberry or raspberry preserves. I frost a layer then pipe a "dam" of frosting around the perimeter of it before spooning in the fruit filling. When I'm done stacking, it's time to crumb-coat the cake (add a thin layer of frosting). Then I put it in the fridge for about half an hour. When it's chilled, I remove it from the fridge, add eight to ten Boba straws or dowels that have been cut to the exact height of the cake. Then I add my final layer of frosting and decorate in whatever style the bride has requested. I repeat this process for my 9-inch cakes and 6-inch cakes. I rarely put the cake layers together until I get to the reception hall. (I've had cakes fall over in the car on the way to the event!) When I'm ready to stack my tiers, I pipe a buttercream trim across the seams then run a dowel down through the center of all three cakes for stability. Most wedding cakes are topped with flowers or some sort of wedding topper. And there you have it—a beautiful tiered wedding cake!

P.S. What About That Naked Cake?

To make a "naked" cake, I add a thin crumb-coat and then scrape most of the icing off. The cake isn't completely "naked," but I do allow bits of the cake to peek through. It might seem a bit odd at first, but when it's all put together and greenery (or fruit) is added, you'll see that the result is pretty amazing. Some folks even sprinkle sifted powdered sugar over their naked cakes at the last minute, coating the berries in a soft white lace. Yum!

Read on for a sneak peek of another exciting book
in the Mysteries of Lancaster County series!

Seek & Ye Shall Find
by DeAnna Dodson

The morning was brisk but not bitter, and even though it was November, the snow wouldn't likely come for a little while yet. Mary Classen Baxter pulled her heavy heather-gray sweater a little more snugly around herself as she rearranged a display of royal-blue Depression glassware, glad the converted barn that contained her family's thrift store and gift shop, Secondhand Blessings, was nice and warm.

It had been quiet in the store so far this Thursday morning, especially with the quilting circle deciding not to meet this week. One tourist couple had come in looking for antique quilts but hadn't bought anything, and as of yet there had been only one other customer, Mrs. Hazeldine. She came in frequently to see if anyone had brought in any flatware that matched her grandmother's set. Mary's oldest sister, Elizabeth, had just gone into the house to see if their middle sister, Martha, needed any help preparing lunch. As usual, Martha would most likely tell Elizabeth she enjoyed cooking for the three of them and was well able to handle everything on her own, but Mary suspected that, this morning in particular, Elizabeth just wanted to make sure Martha was all right.

Elizabeth could always tell when Martha had something weighing heavily on her mind, and Martha had seemed a little down lately.

Mary's thoughts were interrupted by the arrival of two men. One of them appeared to be in his fifties, tall, clean cut, dark hair and eyes, a little gray at the temples. The other looked a lot like him, minus the gray, and looked about half his age. Father and son, she immediately assumed.

The older man approached her with a tentative smile. "Are you Elizabeth Classen?"

"I'm Mary. Elizabeth is my sister. Can I get her for you?"

"I suppose you could help me. Jonas Petersheim sent me over. He said you know him."

"Sure," she said. "My family has known the Petersheims for years. What can I do for you?"

The man hesitated.

"I'm going to look around some," the younger one said, and he headed over to a shelf full of old books.

"Was there something you were looking for in particular?" Mary asked the older man.

"Yeah. Mr. Petersheim, uh, Jonas, said you had a wooden keepsake box his son Noah brought to you to sell on consignment. I'd like to buy it."

"I'd be happy to show it to you."

She took him over to a table with several handmade wooden items on display, including some very lovely boxes that would have been ideal for jewelry or other small trinkets. She showed him the one Noah Petersheim had brought to her that past summer. It was a small box, elegant in its simplicity, with a glass-smooth finish. He picked it up gingerly.

"Whoever made it spent a lot of time on it," she said.

"Yeah, he must have." The man looked at it for a long moment, not opening it, obviously thinking about more than the box itself, and then he gave her a half-embarrassed smile. "I'm sorry, it's just— Uh, maybe I'd better introduce myself. I'm Dean Flynn, and that's my son, Riley."

"Good to meet you," Mary said. The man still hadn't opened the box, so she added, "It's very nice on the inside too."

The corner of his mouth twitched up slightly, but he finally lifted the lid. There was a divided tray that fit at the top of the box, and after a moment, he lifted that out, revealing the larger space below.

"I'm surprised it hasn't sold before now," Mary said. "It's one of the prettiest I've ever seen, and the price isn't bad at all."

"No," he said, still seeming to be thinking of something besides what was in front of him. "No, it's very nice. Maybe it hasn't sold yet because it was meant for me."

"Maybe so," Mary said cheerfully. "Of course, we have several others to choose from too, if you're interested in something different. The one on the end there is—"

"No. Thanks a lot, but I actually came for this one. Mr., uh, Jonas said you might still have it."

"I'm glad we do. So, do you want me to wrap it up for you?"

"I'd like that very much." He glanced over at his son who was investigating an antique set of the complete works of

Charles Dickens. "But no hurry. It looks like Riley isn't quite ready to leave yet."

"That's all right. Feel free to look around as much as you'd like." She paused for a moment, knowing Mrs. Hazeldine was listening in as usual, and then let her curiosity get the better of her. "Have you known the Petersheims long?"

"I don't know them at all, actually. I just met Jonas today, him and his son. I'd like to meet the rest of them, if there are any. I think." He looked over at his son again and then back at Mary. "Could I ask you something?"

"Uh, sure. I can't promise I know the answer, but you can go ahead and ask."

"I'm just wondering what you can tell me about the Petersheims."

She nodded toward the vintage table and chairs set up nearby. "Why don't we sit down for a minute? As long as your son is looking around."

"Okay. Thanks. I don't mean to monopolize your time or anything, but some information would sure be welcome." He looked around the store and nodded toward Mrs. Hazeldine. "Are you sure you have the time?"

"Certainly. And it's no trouble."

They settled at the table. Dean was still looking at the box, inside and out, almost as if he couldn't believe it was real.

"What did you want to know about the Petersheims?" Mary asked him finally. "I've known them all my life. Not that our families are close, but we're acquainted. With the Reihls too."

"With who?"

"The Reihls. Abigail Reihl was born a Petersheim. She's Jonas's cousin."

"Oh." There wasn't much humor in his soft laugh. "I didn't know about her."

Mary wasn't sure what it was, but something about the way he said that made her feel a little uneasy. "Are you related to the family?"

"Yeah. Jonas is my uncle. My mother, Susan, was his sister."

She raised her eyebrows. She had heard of Susan Petersheim a time or two before. She had supposedly left Bird-in-Hand and married an *Englischer*. The rest of the family never talked about her. "I didn't know she had a son."

There was a touch of wryness in his smile. "I didn't know she was my mother."

She blinked at him.

He looked tired all of a sudden. "It's kind of a long story. My adoptive mother passed away last month, the woman I had always believed was my birth mother. Her attorney gave me a letter she had asked him to hold until she was gone. It told me I had been adopted and who my birth mother was. I can tell you—" He rubbed his eyes. "That's not something I was ready to hear at the age of fifty-one."

"I guess that would be quite a shock," she said. No wonder he looked a little dazed.

"Anyway, that's why I came here. My mom's letter said my birth mother and her husband had been killed in a car accident many years ago. Mom said Susan was originally from Bird-in-Hand. She also said that Susan never had any other children, so I know my only chance at finding any relatives is here. I asked at the gas station if there were still any Petersheims around, and they told me about Jonas. An older lady at the smorgasbord told me that Susan was his sister. I didn't know about the cousin. What did you say her name was?"

"Abigail Reihl."

"Abigail Reihl," he repeated as if he was trying out the name. "I guess I'll try to see her too."

Mary started to say something and then checked herself. Better to let him ask about what he wanted to know and not add any of her own opinions. "So Jonas sent you here?" she asked instead.

Dean nodded, looking at the box he still held. "He said this had been my mother's. I didn't get the impression that he was very happy about his son bringing it here, but I didn't ask him about it. I just wanted to know if he still had anything of hers. He said this was the last. I guess I shouldn't be too surprised at that. It's been over half a century since she lived in Bird-in-Hand."

"This must be very difficult for you."

"It certainly wasn't what I was planning on, but I would like to know more about my family. My real family." He stopped himself. "No, that's not what I mean. My mom and dad, all the rest of the relatives I grew up with, they *are* my real family. But I'd like to know where I came from too. I'd like to know about my birth mother and why she gave me away." He pressed his lips tightly together then said, "I just need to know what happened."

"I wish I could tell you," Mary said gently. "But this was all before my time."

"Yeah. I'd guess she left here at least a decade before you were born."

She laughed, more than a little bit pleased that he thought she was so young. "No, probably the same year. If you're fifty-one, I'm only a year younger than you."

"You're kidding me. No way."

"I'm afraid so, but thanks for not believing me."

He glanced at her left hand, pretending not to, and she couldn't help the touch of warmth that rose to her cheeks. He wasn't wearing a wedding ring either. Divorced? Widowed? It might be nice to find out, but he was probably only interested in finding out about whatever family he had in the area.

"Anyway," he said, catching her eye and then looking a little flustered himself, "I'd appreciate any information you can give me, and if you'd tell me where my mother's cousin lives, I'd appreciate that too. Between Jonas Petersheim and Abigail Reihl, I ought to be able to find out a lot about my mother. That's what I came for."

"Sure." Mary glanced over at his son again. He seemed to be looking through an old collection of Agatha Christies now. He'd probably be a while. "Umm, let me see," she said to Dean. "If you met Jonas, you know they're Amish, but I'm afraid his only direct family is his son, Noah. His wife passed away when Noah was young, and Jonas never remarried. Noah has always stayed on to run the farm. That's the easy side of the family."

Dean looked amused and encouraged her to go on.

"Then there's Abigail Reihl. Her husband passed away last year. They have three daughters and a son, a lot of grand-children, and even more great-grandchildren. The son and his family moved to Philadelphia, but most of the rest of them still live around here. Abigail loves telling people about them, especially the little ones, but you might as well know up front that she doesn't usually care to talk to newcomers very much. It took her a while to open up to me when I came back to Bird-in-Hand, and I was born here."

"Wow. Maybe I ought to arrange for an introduction instead of just showing up, huh?"

He looked at her appealingly, and she couldn't help smiling.

"I guess I could go out there with you and see what she says." Mary cringed a little bit inside. What would her sisters say if she went off somewhere with a man she'd just met? Even if it was just to Abigail Reihl's? Maybe a little bit of caution was in order. "Let me just go in and get my sister, so she can look after the store for me. I'll be right back."

She found Martha and Elizabeth both in the kitchen. Martha was standing over the antique stove stirring a pot of stew while Elizabeth set out bowls and spoons. Their dachshund was asleep in her basket in the corner. From the tantalizing smell, Mary knew there was a loaf of oat bread baking. She was suddenly ravenous.

"I'm sorry to hear that," Elizabeth was saying. "I would have loved to see them."

"See who?" Mary asked.

Martha sighed. "I was afraid it was going to turn out like this, but I just found out for sure that neither of my boys can come for Thanksgiving this year. It's just going to be Trish and her family."

"Aww, really?" Mary gave her a sympathetic pat. "Neither of your boys is coming? That's too bad, especially since neither of mine can make it either. And I would have loved to see my little Nicky again."

"You just spent time with your new grandbaby," Elizabeth protested with a smile.

"What?" Mary asked. "There's a limit?"

Elizabeth laughed, but Martha's somber expression didn't change. "Who's minding the store?" she asked.

"Mrs. Hazeldine's in there," Mary said. "She'll keep an eye on things for a minute. There are only two other customers, and I need to talk to you about them."

Elizabeth pulled out a chair and sat down. Martha tapped her wooden spoon on the rim of the stew pot before putting it on the spoon rest, startling the orange tabby cat dozing in the kitchen window, and then sat down as well.

Mary smiled as she looked at her sisters. The three of them were so different, and yet together they made a great combination, balancing out each other's strengths and weaknesses, better for their different abilities and experiences.

Martha turned her head a little to one side and narrowed her eyes, her lips pursed. "Is something wrong?"

"No," Mary said. "Not wrong. It's a long story, and I really shouldn't go into it right now, but a man and his son came into the store looking for something Noah Petersheim brought in. Turns out he's Jonas Petersheim's nephew, and he wants to meet Abigail Reihl."

"His nephew?" Martha said. "I didn't know he had one."

"Evidently he didn't know it either. He's adopted. Anyway, you know how Abigail is. I thought this man would do better if he had someone local introduce him to her, so I'm going to go over with them."

"I'm sure you're right about the introduction," Elizabeth admitted, "but I don't think I like you driving off with two men we've never seen before."

"It's a terrible idea," Martha said. "You can give them directions out to Abigail's. It's not hard to find."

Mary huffed. "Lizzie can come meet them and make sure they're okay. She can even take down their license plate number. Then they'd at least know somebody besides me knows I took them to meet Abigail."

Martha crossed her arms. "Absolutely not. What good would identifying them do if you had already been killed?"

"They just need a little help," Mary said. "It's no big deal."

They both looked at Elizabeth who was shaking her head. "How about something that's not crazy but still helpful?"

Martha smiled.

"If that'll make you feel better," Mary said, lifting her chin.

"Okay then." Elizabeth got up. "What if I go back to the shop with you and meet them?" She glanced at Martha. "And memorize their license plate number and what kind of car they're driving?"

Martha frowned.

"And then," Elizabeth continued, "what if you drove your own car over to Abigail's and let them follow you in theirs?" Again, she glanced at Martha, one eyebrow raised. "No harm in that, right?"

Martha nodded reluctantly. "I suppose not. Just don't be all day about it." She went back to the stove and picked up her wooden spoon. "Lunch will be ready in about an hour."

"Keep it hot for us," Mary said as she grabbed Elizabeth's hand and pulled her out of the kitchen.

"Make sure you take your phone," Elizabeth said right before they went back into the store.

Mary smiled as she led the way to the table. "This is my sister Elizabeth," she said. "Elizabeth, this is Dean Flynn and his son, Riley."

Riley had come to join his father at the table, bringing with him several old books he had decided to buy. Elizabeth shook hands with both men.

"Jonas sent me out to see you," Dean told her, "but your sister here has been very helpful."

"I'm glad," Elizabeth said with her usual graciousness. "I understand you want to meet Abigail Reihl."

"That's my hope. I guess your sister told you why I'm here." He put his hand on the keepsake box again. "I have a lot of questions."

There was understanding and sympathy now in Elizabeth's eyes. "I'm sure Mary would be happy to introduce you to her. I was just talking to our other sister, Martha. She said we wouldn't be having lunch for another hour or so. I'm sure that's plenty of time for Mary to lead you over to the Reihl place." She looked at Mary significantly.

Mary got her purse from behind the counter. "Call me if you need anything while I'm out. Otherwise, I'll be back for lunch."

"Thanks for helping us out," Dean said. He turned to Riley as they both got up from the table. "Are you buying those?"

Riley nodded.

"I'll get them for you," his father said. "You ought to get something out of this trip."

"I'm happy to come with you, Dad. You shouldn't have to do this by yourself." Riley picked up the books and the box, and they all headed over to the counter to complete the sale. Before they got there, Riley caught his foot on the corner of an old rug and stumbled, sending the books and the box flying.

"Oh, man," he said as he scrambled to pick everything up. "That was klutzy."

"No harm done," Mary said as she and Elizabeth helped gather the books.

Dean went to where the box was lying on its side. The lid was hanging open, and the inside tray had skittered under a nearby chair. He picked everything up but didn't put the tray back where it belonged. Instead, he was staring into the box, his expression puzzled.

"What is it, Dad?" Riley asked.

"I think I should have looked in here a little more carefully."

Dean carried the box to the counter, and all four of them looked inside. In the bottom, a small wooden panel, invisible when it was in place, had popped loose. Dean lifted it out, exposing a folded piece of paper. He took that out too.

"That looks old," his son said. "What is it?"

Dean carefully unfolded it and began to read, looking more and more baffled as he did.

"What is it?" Riley asked again.

"I'm not sure." He looked shaken as he passed it over to Mary and Elizabeth. "Do you know where this is?"

Elizabeth studied the paper, and Mary read it over her shoulder. It was clearly a deed, and it was dated nearly forty years earlier. Mary didn't recognize the legal description of the property, but she did know the address that went with it.

"That's Jonas Petersheim's place," she said. She looked to see whose name was on the deed, and her mouth dropped open.

Dean pointed to the paper. "And the deed is made out to me."

A NOTE FROM THE EDITORS

We hope you enjoyed this volume of the Mysteries of Lancaster County series, created by the Books and Inspirational Media Division of Guideposts. We are a nonprofit organization that touches millions of lives every day through products and services that inspire, encourage, help you grow in your faith, and celebrate God's love in every aspect of your daily life.

Thank you for making a difference with your purchase of this book, which helps fund our many outreach programs to military personnel, prisons, hospitals, nursing homes, and educational institutions. To learn more, visit GuidepostsFoundation.org.

We also maintain many useful and uplifting online resources. Visit Guideposts.org to read true stories of hope and inspiration, access OurPrayer network, sign up for free newsletters, download free e-books, join our Facebook community, and follow our stimulating blogs.

To learn about other Guideposts publications, including the bestselling devotional *Daily Guideposts*, go to ShopGuideposts .org, call (800) 932-2145, or write to Guideposts, PO Box 5815, Harlan, Iowa 51593.

Find more inspiring fiction in these best-loved Guideposts series!

Secrets of Wayfarers Inn
Fall back in history with three retired schoolteachers who find themselves owners of an old warehouse-turned-inn that is filled with hidden passages, buried secrets and stunning surprises that will set them on a course to puzzling mysteries from the Underground Railroad.

Sugarcreek Amish Mysteries
Be intrigued by the suspense and joyful "aha" moments in these delightful stories. Each book in the series brings together two women of vastly different backgrounds and traditions, who realize there's much more to the "simple life" than meets the eye.

Mysteries of Martha's Vineyard
Come to the shores of this quaint and historic island and dig into a cozy mystery. When a recent widow inherits a lighthouse just off the coast of Massachusetts, she finds exciting adventures, new friends, and renewed hope.

Patchwork Mysteries
Discover that life's little mysteries often have a common thread in a series where every novel contains an intriguing mystery centered around a quilt located in a beautiful New England town.

Mysteries of Silver Peak
Escape to the historic mining town of Silver Peak, Colorado, and discover how one woman's love of antiques helps her solve mysteries buried deep in the town's checkered past.

**To learn more about these books,
visit Guideposts.org/Shop**

Sign up for the
Guideposts Fiction Newsletter
and stay up to date on the books you love!

You'll get sneak peeks of new releases, recommendations from other Guideposts readers, and special offers just for you . . .
and it's FREE!

Just go to Guideposts.org/Newsletters today to sign up.

Guideposts.

Visit Guideposts.org/Shop
or call (800) 932-2145